A Short Life

on

A Sunny Isle

The sun has set,

and trees,

like statues,

meditate.

Garcia Lorca

by Hannah Blank

The Alphonse Dantan Mysteries

A MURDER OF CONVENIENCE (1999)

BRAVE MAN DEAD (2001)

A SHORT LIFE ON A SUNNY ISLE (2002)

Non-Fiction

MASTERING MICROS (1983)

DON'T GO: 51 Reasons Not to Travel Abroad,
BUT IF YOU MUST: 176 Tactics for Coping With
Discomforts, Distress and Danger (1996)

Hannah Blank

A Short Life

on

A Sunny Isle

An Alphonse Dantan Mystery

Hightrees Books
Imprint of Prism Corporation
New York

Published by Hightrees Books,
        an Imprint of Prism Corporation
    New York, New York 10021

Library of Congress Catalog Card Number: 2002109488

Blank, Hannah
A Short Life on A Sunny Isle /
Hannah Blank

p.cm.

ISBN 0-9652778-4-4

Printed in the United States of America

10 9 8 7 6 5 4 3 2 1

For my husband Leonard, again

TABLE OF CONTENTS

HISTORICAL NOTE

The Spain of fifty years ago was a different world than the Spain of today. In those days the Spanish people lived under an oppressive regime, a fascist dictatorship headed by Generalissimo Francisco Franco. Many people were poor and uneducated. They were controlled at every turn; they could not bear arms; their reading, their movies, were censored and restricted. The works of one of the nation's greatest poets, Garcia Lorca, were banned from bookstores; he had been a Communist before being assassinated by the Fascists. The citizens were surrounded in the streets by weapons-carrying soldiers and Guardia Civil perhaps more numerous than the population at large, but the ordinary citizen could not own a weapon, and therefore had no hope of overthrowing the oppressors. Women were expected to stay home caring for their families and teaching their children strict, very strict, religious principles. Their husbands sought evening recreation at restaurants and dancing, but with women who were not their wives.

There was little commerce; a big export was Valencian oranges. Even tourism, in this land of incomparable art and natural, if austere, beauty, was very light. This was in part because Europeans couldn't afford to travel that much in those years, and American travellers were still discovering Paris and Rome and had not started seeking farther afield. But it was partly because the support systems to capture and engage and accommodate foreign travellers were not in place.

Although Mallorca in the Balearic Islands was somewhat known and visited (after all, everyone knew of the romantic interlude spent in Palma de Mallorca by Frederic Chopin and George Sand), the other islands in the chain were largely undiscovered; difficult to reach, and with few amenities. A few foreigners eager to live very cheaply had learned of Ibiza and Formentera and the other islands by word-of-mouth.

Today Spain is a bustling prosperous modern industrialized democracy; and a worthy member of the Western world. And Ibiza, like Mallorca, is a luxurious perch for the glitterati.

CAST OF CHARACTERS

OLD FRIENDS:

Alphonse Dantan - an Inspector at the Paris
Police Judiciare
Judy Dantan - his irrepressible American wife
Miri Winter - their young American friend who
went to Ibiza to "paint"
Seymour Levin - Miri's sometimes boyfriend, just
being discharged from the U.S. Army

BRITISH:

Nigel - de facto group leader of the expatriates
Pamela - Nigel's plump dimpled love sometimes
called "Dumples"
Dorcas & Hazel - aging, bridge-playing
"Saphists"
Edgar & Percy - cat-lovers whom Max has
dubbed "Twit & Twerp"
Lady Mary - a real "Lady," dignified even when
drunk: "Lady Lush"

AUSTRALIAN:

Mavis - world-weary, whose lover, Vicente, is an
Ibizan fisherman

BELGIAN:

Hugo - nicknamed "The Belch"

SWEDISH:

Jorgen - sculptor, redbearded giant nicknamed "The Great Dane"

AMERICAN:

Harriet - middle-aged gossip from the Midwest
Max - foul-mouthed writer known to beat his girlfriend Francine
Fred - artist and womanizer
Cindy - Fred's wife

GERMAN:

Ilse & Hans - owners of the *Fonda Bahia*, possibly former Nazis
Lotte & Leo - artists, escapees from Nazi Germany

FRENCH:

Francine - poetess, Max's battered girlfriend
Claude - recent arrival, wants to open a dockside restaurant for tourists
Denise - friend of Claude's - travel-agent

IBIZANS:

Liberto - owner of cafe frequested by expatriates
Tomas Bonet - 21-year-old son of well-to-do merchant accused by police of murder
Catalina Bonet - Tomas' 16-year-old sister
Inez Bonet - Tomas' cousin who works at a family shop
Inez' father - drunken house-agent
Maria Figuera - 14-year-old maid at the *fonda* - the murder victim
Consuelo Figuera - Maria's 15-year-old sister, also a maid at the *fonda*
doctor - the only one in San Marino
butcher - owner of the ice-house
Pedro - restaurant owner
Pedro's staff of waiters and cooks and cleaners
Pedro's garbage-man
Teresa - peasant who cleans houses for some expatriates
Teresa's young daughter - lingering of a long-standing unknown illness
Vicente - fisherman, unable to speak any of the languages his love Mavis knows

PRELUDE

THE DANTANS AT HOME

It was early August 1955. Inspector Alphonse Dantan of the Paris *Police Judiciare* had satisfactorily concluded an investigation during which he had been away from his young American wife many hours of the night, every night. All the characters in the Paginot case had been night-people; most of his inquiries and interviews had had to take place long after sunset. Judy had nagged him for weeks that he was not spending enough time with her while he was working on the Paginot case.

Now that his role in the case was over and they could have spent more time together, perversely, Judy decided to take a trip by herself. She was going to visit her friend, Miri Winter, in Spain, where the latter had gone to paint. Perhaps Judy wanted show him how it felt to be lonely now that he had time to be so. But Dantan found that he was rather pleased at the prospect of being on his own in Paris for a week or so. His pal from work, Jean-Jacques Pilieu, an inveterate bachelor, had volunteered to work while many members of the P.J. would be on vacation for the month of August. Dantan had also volunteered to stay around. Just being off the Paginot case was vacation enough, and his wife's planned sojourn without him added to his carefree feeling.

A chance encounter with a former *amie* had led him to a bit of daydreaming. Her manner had been coquettish; inviting. He felt a slight hankering for something different, but so far had not pursued the temptation.

"When are you planning to leave for Ibiza?" Dantan asked his wife at dinner one Sunday evening. Germaine, the couple's maid and cook, had produced an excellent *coq au vin* that morning before her half-day off, and Judy had managed to re-heat on her shiny expensive German range. He was feeling a sense of well-being.

The Dantans always took their meals at the great antique mahogany table Judy had purchased from Jean-Jacques' mother. It made her feel more

European than eating at the charming breakfast-nook her father had had built in their kitchen along with the many other thousands of francs of renovations and installations Mister Kugel had provided for his only daughter.

"As soon as Luigi has finished dying the six pairs of sandals he made to match the linen sheaths I had made for the trip – pink, yellow, baby blue, pale green, white, and beige. Probably in about a week. Anyway, I don't want to get there until after that festival that Miri wrote me about is over. Something about Ibizans celebrating the victory over the Moors a lot of centuries ago. I'm not interested in native festivals."

"You won't need to be *chic* there. Just take some shorts and shirts," Dantan advised her.

"Shorts don't flatter me."

Dantan rose from his chair long enough to pat her rump amiably. "You have a *derrière charmante.*"

Judy giggled, but remained determined to have all new outfits for her trip.

"How long are you going to stay?"

"I'm not sure. Maybe it will be too hot in San Marino. And maybe it will be too uncomfortable at Miri's house. She has no running water unless it is pumped first, and no hot water at all unless she boils it on the coal-stove. But maybe I'll love it, the beach and the shopping and meeting all those oddballs who Miri says live there. I'm also hoping Miri will help me discover a really talented unknown artist so I can buy a good painting at a bargain price. Since Miri left Paris I haven't added a single painting to my collection.

"And I also want to shop for things they make there. I've heard about Mallorcan mother-of-pearl embroidery, straw hats and bags all very cheap, hand-knit sweaters and shawls, maybe even baby things embroidered in miniscule stitches by the local nuns."

Dantan was interested to hear this last item but asked no questions. "Don't buy so much that I have to come down there to help you bring it back!" He laughed.

He knew his wife's unfettered self-indulgence, fostered by a pair of rich worshipful parents. He couldn't complain too much about them, however, for if they had not been so indulgent with their daughter it was probable they would have interfered with the marriage, which was not the kind of match they had envisioned for their baby. But they always had found it nearly impossible to deny her anything.

The Kugels had been exceedingly generous to the newlyweds, buying them a spacious apartment in a lovely neighborhood of Paris near the Luxembourg Gardens, and spending a fortune to rehabilitate it to its former elegance and modernize it with powerful wiring and formidable foreign appliances.

"Alphie, would you like to come with me?"

"Do you want me to?"

Judy giggled. "This visit is for gossiping and shopping. From what Miri has written, there isn't much else to do. You would be bored."

For a couple married less than two years* there was always something to do. But he merely said, "I certainly don't want to be bored."

*Alphonse and Judy met and married in Paris in the first Alphonse Dantan mystery, A MURDER OF CONVENIENCE [Hightrees Books, 1999]

ONE

LAZY LIBERTO'S

Miri had gone to the village for morning coffee as usual, riding her Velo-Solex to within an inch of the palm tree in front of Lazy Liberto's, the cafe by the water preferred by the expatriates. The tiny motor on the front wheel of her sturdy bicycle made all the difference in the heat of sweating up the hills toward her house, and getting there with relative ease.

The Belch's green Vespa, with its capacious shopping basket attached at the rear, was already beside the palm tree. The basket was empty. After having coffee with the group, Hugo, a Flemish Belgian, would often load up at the local store with imported canned ham, cheeses, pastries and choco late-bars to secrete in his room, despite three ample meals a day available at the *Fonda Bahia*, the boarding-house run by the German couple, Hans and Ilse. He had a weakness for the ultra-sweet Spanish chocolate, and was forever trying to devise new ways to keep it from melting in the heat, from buying a block of ice each morning and stashing it in the washbasin in his room to wrapping the chocolate in many layers of newspapers for insulation. Sometimes, when the chocolate was on the verge of liquefying, he offered it around to the expatriates at Liberto's. If it was too far gone, he gave it to the maids at the *fonda*.

Four of the expatriate crowd were already sitting at their usual table, the big round one with the Cinzano umbrella. One of them called out to Miri with a laughing, "Luck or skill?" This was Nigel, a good-looking middle-aged Brit who spent a lot of time at Liberto's. He seemed to be the de facto leader among the expatriates.

"Skill, of course," Miri retorted pertly, "since you can't prove otherwise."

Pamela, Nigel's petite blonde lover, not as young as she thought she looked, scowled at the flirting.

Nigel and Pamela had come to San Marino two years before, in 1953, each having left a spouse behind in England. They were among the drinkers and loungers living on the island on independent incomes.

Harriet, a spindly widow from the Midwest, waved Miri into the empty rattan chair on her left. "And how are you this morning, my dear?"

"Okay."

Harriet gave a quick nod at the fat man on her right. "Poor fellow, he seems especially morose this morning."

Miri glanced contemptuously at Hugo, fat and gross, his rear-end overflowing the rattan chair, silently slurping hot chocolate and stuffing himself with *empanadas*. He was disgusting. Max, an American writer with a beard and a sharp tongue had nicknamed him "The Belch."

Max arrived next. He glanced at The Belch with scorn as the latter continued to stuff himself. Max ascetically confined himself to liquids, such as brandy. With a provocative leer he sat himself down next to Miri. She turned away.

Harriet whispered to Miri, "Notice that Francine isn't here?" Max was known to beat his girlfriend Francine, a fragile French poetess. Francine was absent probably because her bruises were too conspicuous to cover up with makeup and sunglasses.

Liberto, putting the lie to the nickname "Lazy" with which Max had dubbed him, was scurrying back and forth ceaselessly with trays of coffee, cognac, *manzanilla,* and *empañadas.* He knew the favorites of all the regulars. The Belge ate a continuous supply of *empañadas.* Pamela sipped black coffee, Harriet, *manzanilla.* Miri drank coffee with hot milk. Max drank brandy all day long. Liberto now dashed out with the brandy for Max and Miri's usual coffee with milk, nearly colliding with a giant of a man with a red beard who strode over to the table as if with eyes closed, or at least, focused on something elsewhere.

He twirled an empty chair from another table and brutishly pushed it between Max and Miri. This was Jorgen, a sculptor, a redhaired giant from Sweden.

"I still want to do your head," Jorgen told Miri gruffly.

"Some other time."

"Then another time."

She still had uncomfortable feelings about Jorgen. About a month before she had been alone in her isolated hill-top house, when she was alarmed to see through the glass French doors a large man with a walking-stick trudging up the scrubby hill. Only when he was banging on the door did she realize who it was. This alarmed her only slightly less.

As she stood there staring at him through the glass he slid the door open himself. "I'm here to see your pictures," he announced, striding into the spacious yet sparsely-furnished main room. Its only seating was a pair of built-in concrete whitewashed benches facing each other by the fireplace. The only other object in the large room was her easel, on which rested a partially completed canvas depicting a rocky beach with a dazzling blue sky. Her finished paintings were propped face in against the walls. Jorgen strode over and turned them around.

Since her arrival on Ibiza four months before, she had been painting brilliantly lit and simply constructed scenes of San Marino: dazzling whitewashed houses flanking narrow winding cobblestone streets, a procession of shapeless women swathed in black entering a blindingly white church, a small fisherman's boat at the wharf, light reflected on the water ....

Jorgen proceeded slowly and silently from one painting to another, scrutinizing each first up close, then stepping back, a long thick finger pressed against his bearded chin. After examining each of the four he pronounced, "travel posters."

Miri's face burned, but she said nothing.

Then he studied her head for a moment and

said, "I would like to do a sculpture of your head." Without waiting for a reply, he left, and she watched him trudge back down the scrubby hill.

She then sat down and cried, something she did not approve of doing, and almost never did. But thinking about it, she admitted to herself that he might have a point; the paintings were too light and bright to mean anything.

For several days after that she was unable to pick up her brushes, and pondered what to do next. Her alternatives were to give up painting altogether or leave San Marino for some gloomier climate where the dazzling sun would not intrude. Then one morning Jorgen mutely drew her away from the group at the cafe and led her to his studio in the basement of the Germans' *fonda*. He shared the basement with the coal furnace where hot water was made for the rooms, heaps of coal, continually replenished by Jose, the coal-stoker, and a primitive laundry where the maids in their black pinafores scrubbed the *fonda's* bed-linens and towels on washboards, rinsed them in tubs, and put them through a hand-turned wringer salvaged from an ancient washing-machine. Jorgen's stone sculptures were all around the space on crudely made pedestals, small tables, and boxes. Human figures, busts, a few animals. Miri found them very interesting.

Although he had a room upstairs in the *fonda* he kept a cot in a corner for resting if he was engrossed in a piece and working for a long stretch. Near the cot was a heap of clothes and a bookshelf on the concrete wall near which held a few old tomes.

Jorgen sat Miri down on a wooden bench, withdrew from a shelf two large books falling-apart with age and use, sat down beside her and began showing her selected pages. They were black-and-white reproductions of the works of Edvard Munch and Kathe Kollwitz. The former book was in Norwegian and the latter, German. Miri was excited by what she saw. These were artists she could learn from!

Soon after that visit she undertook to do a very different kind of painting from her "travel posters."

A local woman, Teresa, who looked fifty but was actually no more than thirty, worked cleaning houses for foreigners. Miri had not felt she needed a maid, but Harriet had persuaded her to give Teresa some work as she was so poor, and had a sick child, bedridden, with an unidentified lingering illness. So for four *pesetas*, or ten cents an hour, Miri hired Teresa to clean for her for a few hours each week. Teresa was one of the Ibicencans who could actually speak

Spanish. Most of the locals only spoke Ibicencan, a dialect of Catalan, but those who came into contact with foreigners picked up some Spanish. Miri and Teresa spent a lot of time talking. Miri couldn't understand how Teresa, and other Ibicencans, could be so resigned to the harshness of their lives. But she couldn't bestir any feelings of rebellion or resistance in Teresa. It was all God's will. Except that in Miri's opinion there was no God, so whose will was it?

Miri visited Maria's house in the fields and saw the sick child in bed. She asked if she could paint her, and insisted on paying Maria four *pesetas* an hour for the time the child "sat" for her.

Miri felt her painting was too much like Munch, but she was glad to have gotten a deeper mood into her work. And she would keep trying. She would have liked to borrow those books from Jorgen but did not do so for two reasons: one, she was afraid that if she looked at them too much her paintings would become too much like theirs; and two, she didn't want to be obligated to Jorgen. Although he hadn't touched her yet, she sensed that it was imminent.

Nigel and Pamela were talking with Max, whom they seemed to find amusing, and Jorgen, whom they liked. The ignored the others. It was clear that Harriet bored them, the Belge disgusted them, and Miri was too naive for their taste. They were angry, too, that in her innocence she had captured the house on the hill which had been boarded up for years.

All the expatriates, at one time or another, had tried to rent this house, and Nigel had tried the hardest, but each was rebuffed by its drunken agent, *Señor* Bonet. Then Miri appeared on the scene; *Señor* Bonet treated her like a princess and gladly rented her the house.

The secret was that Miri had treated him with respect, despite his staggering inebriation, and had not insulted him with attempts at blandishments and bribes, as had the others.

Miri had been directed to the agent by his young daughter Inez, who was tending a roadside stand at which Miri had stopped for a soda while biking between the capital of Ibiza (also called Ibiza) and San Marino, one of the villages more favored by foreigners. Miri told her, as she told everyone, she was looking for a house in San Marino.

"My father is the agent for one," Inez said, and told Miri in which bars in Ibiza to look for her father.

The next to arrive at Liberto's were Mavis and Claude.

Mavis, a worn-looking middle-aged Australian, had been wandering the earth feeling rootless until she found Ibiza, whose remoteness, serenity and primitiveness encouraged her to feel she might be able to settle there. She began a passionate affair with a local fisherman, with whom she could barely communicate. Vicente was illiterate, couldn't even speak Spanish, only Ibicencan. Mavis spoke only English and French.

Mavis was seriously thinking of settling in San Marino permanently. She had bought a piece of land, in a field isolated from the village, but near enough to hook up to the village's electricity, and was thinking of having a house built there. But that project had not yet begun. She was renting a small house up the hill in the village. Vicente had been seen visiting there, sending shivers of excitement through the local women, who whispered over this shocking behavior.

In a quiet way Mavis had also become friendly with Claude. He seemed to find her interesting. Alex had made cracks about "older women," until it was learned that Mavis was only four years older than Claude. She appeared to be more.

Claude was a recent arrival to the expatriate

colony. The Frenchman was tall, rangy, sandy-haired, about thirty-five. He had immediately been taken up by the in-crowd because he was charming, but his reason for coming to the island, and to San Marino in particular, was a sore point with many of them.

Claude was known to be considering whether or not San Marino was a suitable place for opening a real French restaurant. Palma de Mallorca, a bustling magnet for tourists, would definitely be more suitable, but Claude liked the *ambiance* of San Marino, its simplicity and calm.

"Exactly what he will destroy if he ever opens that bloody restaurant," Max had rasped when he first heard the idea.

Claude saw an excellent French restaurant as an attraction, not only for the expatriates, whose numbers were slowly growing, but for groups of French tourists who would hear about it and perhaps even make the overnight boat trip from Mallorca to Ibiza to dine "*chez Claude.*" Claude already owned a small delightful restaurant favored in his own Paris neighborhood, but there he was only one of many *restaurateurs*, and business was not booming.

He even had a potential location for his new venture staked out. This was Pedro's, a restaurant situated opposite the fishermen's wharf.

Claude had learned that he could acquire the place very cheaply, and Pedro would be willing to work for him as manager. Claude thought it would be an excellent location for a good French restaurant. It was flanked by a bar frequented by fishermen on one side, and a fishermen's supply store selling nets, ropes, anchors and other small-boat paraphernalia on the other. He thought the French tourists he was sure to attract would find the setting *charmant*.

Nigel and Pamela gave Mavis and Claude a warm welcome. Harriet whispered to Miri, "I wonder if she will drop that unsuitable liaison with the fisherman, and take up with Claude?"

"She's older than he is," Miri whispered back. They were both old as far as Miri, who was only twenty-five, could see, so maybe it didn't matter.

"What have you two been up to?" Max asked jovially. He seemed to have been speculating on the same thing.

"We had dinner at Pedro's last night," Mavis said, pleased to be asked. "The food was wonderful. And a group of fishermen were having a party at the wharf. I spotted Vicente laughing and drinking wine with the other fishermen. But he didn't see me, and I didn't greet him for fear of embarassing him among his friends."

"Suppose Claude had put his restaurant here?" Pamela said quietly, ignoring the fact that Claude was right beside her. "The Ibizan fishermen would not unselfconsciously carouse like that if tourists were gaping at them."

"I'm glad they were enjoying themselves," Harriet said. "They usually look so weary."

That's right, Miri thought suddenly. Maybe she should do a painting of one of the fishermen in his little boat. She could ask Mavis to ask Vicente if he or one of the others would sit for her.

The next to arrive at the morning gathering were the former art students Lotte and Leo, German Jews branded with tattoos on their arms who had escaped from Nazi concentration camps not long before the Liberation. Making their way to Italy, they had met each other among the other Jews gathering to dodge the British blockade and escape by boat to Palestine. They had married, and eventually moved to Ibiza, where living was very cheap. They were surviving on a small stipend from an American relative whom they had never met. He had not offered to help them get to the United States, but sent them money monthly, enough to live on in a cheap place like Portugal or Spain. Both had taken up painting again. Miri had been allowed to visit their house to see their paintings. She could not tell one artist's work from the other. Both produced power-ful and frightening canvassses.

They did not ask to see Miri's work.

Last to arrive were Fred, an American painter and his wife Cindy. Fred was a flirt and a woman-izer, but his bossy curlyhaired wife kept a close watch on him.

Cindy also disliked Miri. Fred had invited Miri to his home to see his paintings (chaperoned by Cindy at all times) and she had expressed enthu-siasm for his work, which she thought emulated Jack-son Pollock. Fred would spill paint all over a rug-sized canvas, the red tile floor, and himself. Miri had been invited several times to see him at work and each time had been effusive. The other painters in the crowd, Lotte and Leo, were less flattering. "He's imitative."

"Using the same technique as another art-ist," Cindy would defend, "is not imitative. It's do-ing what's suitable for the vision. After all, painters through the centuries have been applying paint with brushes. Does that make all of them imitative of the ones before?"

Miri agreed.

Miri disturbed Cindy. She knew that her tall,

dark and handsome husband, always in pursuit of a fresh female conquest, liked to chase young female tourists travelling alone or in pairs. Miri, in town for a more than a tourist's week or two, was a much bigger threat.

Cindy and Fred often came for coffee at Liberto's. Although Cindy didn't much care for sitting around and gossiping, she came to keep an eye on her husband, who loved to hang out, gossip, and ogle other women.

There were other regulars who hadn't showed up yet and those that were there were gossiping about the absentees when the chatter and joking were suddenly interrupted.

TWO

TOMAS

A girl of about sixteen, Catalina Bonet, the daughter of a prosperous local merchant, rushed over to their table, very agitated.

Catalina was well-known to the expatriate community, all of whom shopped at her father's general store, where she helped out behind the counter. She was pretty, outgoing, friendly and helpful, and they all liked her. Her English was fluent, taught by her older brother Tomas, who had been educated in Barcelona at the British Institute.

"*Señores, señoras,* please help me!"

Jorgen pulled over an empy chair from another table and motioned for her to sit down and explain.

"My brother Tomas is suspected of killing a young girl, Maria Figuera, who works at the *Fonda Bahia*! He is innocent, I swear it!"

"Killed?" exclaimed Pamela. "What happened? And why do they think Tomas did it?"

Miri squirmed at the thought of Tomas. He was a dark and sensuous young man of twenty-one who several weeks earlier had forced himself on her. She had exchanged a few words with him from time to time when she went to buy something in his father's general-store, but nothing that she could recall afterwards that had been flirtatious or inviting. She did find his looks pleasantly virile, but hadn't let him know it. Nevertheless, one night he had rumbled up the scrubby hill on his motorcycle, and with very little conversation (she couldn't even remember what he had said), he took her in his arms and began kissing her passionately, then caressing her breasts and body with extreme force. She tried to push him away, but he was overpowering. At some point, she stopped fighting him. He dragged her into her little bedroom, and removing his pants while holding her down on her bed, went all the way. Miri was overcome by excitement more than anger, and began to realize she was enjoying it, and even making rhythmic movements to enhance the feelings.

After they both fell back panting, she felt guilty that she had allowed another man to arouse feelings she had thought she was reserving for Seymour Levin.

Not that anything was going to come of that now, she had a botched a nice thing. But an Ibizan! They were nothing in the world. She couldn't let herself get involved with Tomas. However, she had to ruefully admit to herself that nothing trumped naked lust – as long as it lasted.

He hugged and kissed her a lot before leaving. As he and his motorcycle rumbled down the hill, she called to him repeatedly, "*No mas*! No more! Don't come back!"

If he did, she was afraid she would be lost to a civilized life, the way Mavis was. There was no way she would get involved with someone that would stick her on this backward island, no matter how sensual and overpowering, and how well he spoke English.

Miri's musing about the past was cut short as Catalina blurted out a terrible tale. Her brother Tomas had gone to the pier very early that morning and had found Maria lying on the ground beside his truck. He assumed that the fourteen-year-old girl was unconscious so he immediately drove her to the one doctor in San Marino. Now the local police were seeking to arrest Tomas. They suspected him of murder because he had found the body.

"That's ridiculous!" exclaimed Nigel. "Just because he found the body?"

"Tomas is an upstanding educated intelligent young man," Harriet declared. "He couldn't have done such a thing."

"He went to school in Barcelona at the British Institute," Pamela said. "His English is perfect. And his manners are impeccable."

Except, Miri thought, when he barges in and grabs you.

The maid who answered Tomas' knock told him apologetically that she had strict orders that the doctor could not be disturbed too early in the morning – it was not yet seven. The doctor was still sleeping. Tomas, who was holding the limp body of the young girl in his arms, tried to persuade the maid of the urgency of seeing the doctor but the maid only repeated that she had been ordered not to disturb the doctor before his usual time to arise.

Tomas felt he had no choice but to leave Maria's slight form in the doctor's hallway. He placed her gently on a throne-like carved mahogany chair with instructions to the maid, who stared at him sullenly, that the doctor was to examine the girl as soon as possible.

Tomas considered for a moment storming up the stairs himself to find the doctor's bedroom and rouse him, but the man was so arrogant he might turn his anger on the girl and not treat her properly, especially since she was only a peasant. The doctor might be incompetent – it was rumored that this was so – but he was the only one they had in San Marino. Nobody among the local population seemed to question it when anyone died under his care.

Before driving off he stopped at home to tell his father what had happened and to ask him to follow up to make sure the doctor attended to the girl. Then he drove off to town to carry out his errands.

About two hours later, after Catalina and her father had arrived in the store, the two *Guardia Civil* who were assigned to patrol San Marino came in looking for Tomas. Maria Figuera was dead, they said. They were sure Tomas was their killer and they intended to arrest him. They told *Senor* Bonet that the doctor had reported to them that Tomas had delivered the body of the young girl dead, and that the youg man had acted very suspiciously.

"Why? Because he tried to get medical attention from a son-of-a-bitch too lazy to stir his bones out of bed?" Max said, outraged.

"Maybe she was still alive when the doctor got around to looking at her," said Cindy, "but he is so incompetent that he probably killed her himself." Cindy had been nearly killed herself by the doctor, to whom she had gone with a female complaint. He wanted to remove her appendix, the one operation, apparently, he knew how to perform. One local boy was known to have died under his knife. The gossip was that the doctor had used unclean tools.

Fortunately for Cindy, she and Fred could afford a trip to Barcelona to consult a more competent doctor, who, although beastly to her, made a correct diagnosis and proper prescription for cure. Fred and Cindy then proceeded to take advantage of their trip to Barcelona, visiting many of the Gaudi sites before they left, and raved about them when they returned. Miri promised herself a trip to Barcelona to see the Gaudis as soon as she could get some decent paintings done.

Catalina was in tears. "It's a terrible mistake! Won't somebody take me to town to look for Tomas, warn him and get him to hide?" She looked imploringly at the Belge, who was the only one there with his own vehicle. But he turned his head away. Fred spoke up. "I don't think Tomas should hide. It would seem like an admission of guilt."

Leo and Lotte, who knew from bitter experience that the police could be cruel and unjust, disagreed with Fred. Nigel pronounced the Spanish police ignorant bullies from whom Tomas had to be protected. He offered to take Catalina in a taxi to town to look for Tomas and warn him, but where could they help him to hide?

Mavis, who had remained silent throughout Catalina's recital and the ensuing discussion, now spoke up. "I'll ask Vicente to hide Tomas in his boat. But he docks it here in San Marino, so someone will have to bring Tomas back from the city. He won't be able to drive his own truck back. The police may be looking for it." She rose to go in search of Vicente. She told Nigel where he could find Vicente's boat if he were not out fishing.

"Tomas may not want to hide," said Fred. "He's a proud young man."

"Well he ought to be told that the police want to arrest him," said Mavis calmly, "so that he can decide what he wants to do."

Nigel went into the bar to telephone for one of the two taxis in town, and a few minutes later, he and Catalina were picked up by a driver, elderly and unshaven, whose taxi was ancient too. It was a prewar German vehicle which had been so well cared for it had survived years of rattling on rocky unpaved roads and running over chickens. The tires, however, were completely bald.

Jorgen leaped into the taxi with them "in case another man is needed."

Pamela then joined them, too. "It could hurt Catalina's reputation to be seen riding around with two men, not relations, without a chaperone."

Those remaining at the table were abuzz. Murder on Ibiza was virtually unheard of, except for an occasional newborn found in the fields. No attempt was ever made to identify the mother. None of the peasant women would talk, and if any of them had been pregnant, it would not have been noticed, swathed as they were in yards and yards of heavy black cloth over their heads and rotund forms.

"Tomas probably did do it," Max grumbled, to the vociferous disagreement of the rest of the crowd. "If he hadn't, why would her body be found beside his truck?"

The Belch mumbled what might have been an agreement.

"There could be lots of reasons," said Harriet, but nobody paid any attention to her.

THREE

A CALL FOR HELP

Miri, without a word to the others, left the table and strolled over to the post office across the small plaza, just a few steps away from the cafe. She had an idea for helping Tomas. What Tomas needed (if he was innocent) was a real detective who would know what he was doing, not those illiterate clowns, the *Guardia Civil*, in their black patent leather tricorne hats straight out of a bad operetta. She would ask Judy to ask her husband to come down and solve the case properly. Judy was soon due for a short visit anyway.

At the counter she hestitated only briefly over the blank yellow telegram form before beginning to print vigorously. "JUDY. STOP. TELEPHONE ME

AT HOTEL PALMA LINDA TONIGHT AT SIX.
STOP. URGENT. MIRI. STOP." After reading her
message through, Miri added a "PLEASE," despite
the cost of an additional word. She then handed the
form to the young clerk who began counting words.

The clerk could count words in English or
French, but he couldn't understand them. He knew
that an apostrophe signified a contraction, and therefore should be counted as two words, e.g. "don't"
was two words, "*je t'aime*" three. Max had sent a
telegram to a friend once to test this theory, and it
got through not only the post-office but the censors:
"GO TO HELL, DON'T PASS GO, YOU
FUCKING BASTARD." The clerk had correctly
counted the number of words as ten.

Miri did not want to mention in her telegram
why she wanted Judy to telephone. She was fearful
of the Spanish censors. She didn't want the police
to have the slightest inkling of what she had in mind.
They certainly would not want any *extranjeros* inter-
fering in their official activities. They would not welcome help; the Spanish were too proud to admit
that they could be wrong.

Whether Dantan could overcome these ob-
stacles if he indeed agreed to come to Ibiza with his
wife to poke around into the circumstances of the
crime, she had no idea.

But Miri had faith that if Dantan did come he might think of something.

After sending her telegram, Miri retrieved her Velo-Solex and rode up the bumpy dirt road and around the bay to her house. She wouldn't mention anything to the crowd until she knew for sure that Dantan would be coming with Judy.

She was going to try to paint but at first couldn't get into it.

Miri had gone to paint in San Marino on Ibiza because it was unbelievably inexpensive for non-Spaniards to live there, and was therefore a haven for foreign artists, would-be artists, and ex-patriates who idled there for the sun and the cheap drink.

She had saved enough money at her job in Paris for the U.S. Army* to live on Ibiza for about a year. But after four months, she still was not as productive as she thought she would be.

And she was lonely, something she thought she would never be. She now welcomed hearing from people she could have done without in Paris, such as Judy Dantan.

*Miri was instrumental in bringing in Dantan to solve the murder of a U.S. lieutenant in her Paris office, chronicled in BRAVE MAN DEAD, the second Alphonse Dantan mystery [Hightrees Books, 2001].

Her old boss in Paris, Charlie Nugent, wrote once in awhile to see if she wanted her old job back. And her former boyfriend, soon-to-be discharged Technician 5th Grade, Seymour Levin kept writing in case she wanted to get back together. And of course, she received a postal money order once a month from the Spanish post-office where she had deposited her savings when she left Paris.

That Seymour was "former" was her fault. She had been rude when he tried to get engaged. After an enjoyable affair that lasted eight months, he had had the audacity to buy her a ring (Bohemian garnet) and ask her to marry him. That did it. She was going to be an artist, not a housewife and mother. Maybe someday when she had succeeded as an artist.... How come Seymour hadn't realized that? Piqued, Seymour had misplaced the ring, and took quite awhile to write to her in Spain.

He had written her recently, to tell her that he was (finally!) getting his discharge from the Army, and would be going back to the States in September. In his letter, he asked if she would like him to visit her in Ibiza before he left Europe. She still had not replied.

But when Judy had said she would like to visit, Miri invited her at once. Judy had bored her, but Seymour had importuned her with his incessant requests.

Maybe Judy would talk her in to getting back together with Seymour, against her wishes to be an artist, a career which wasn't going so well in Ibiza.

In the late afternoon, after *siesta*, her maid Teresa arrived, enduring the still-sizzling sun in order to reach the cool house on the hill.

Teresa, who was in her thirties and looked over fifty, worked incessantly, cleaning houses, cleaning at the *fonda*, and working in the fields. Teresa never complained. "*Dios dirá*." Miri didn't want to upset Teresa so she never told her that there was no *Dios*. Why would a loving *Dios* want an innocent child such as Teresa's to die a lingering death? And if there had been a *Dios* he wouldn't have permitted the Nazis to be demonic mass-murderers.

How come their *Dios* didn't want them to be happy and healthy? How come he let Generalissimo Franco seize power and hold the Spanish people in a vise? And never mind all the other cruelties of the past that the Spanish didn't even know about, because most of them had never gotten an education, and certainly had not heard a fair account of history.

Teresa was in a nervous state over the murder, news of which was already spreading throughout the town. Such terrible things never happened in San Marino. Maybe in the capital, Ibiza city – she didn't know, she had never been there – but she had never heard of such a thing.

Miri agreed with her that it was a terrible thing, and incomprehensible.

"She was a good girl," Teresa sighed.

"Everyone who knew her says so."

Teresa dropped her voice to a whisper although there was no one for miles to hear them – except *Dios*, of course. "They're saying Tomas Bonet did it. He has run away. And Maria was in love with him!"

Miri was intrigued. "In love with him! How do you know?"

"She told me one day when I was working at the *fonda*. She wanted advice on whether I thought there was any hope for her with him."

"And did you think there was?"

Teresa shook her head sadly. "Only *Dios* knows."

The house was not really dirty – and Miri really didn't care if it was, the only so-called dirt was sand from the outside – and Teresa was so sad that Miri suggested she earn her pay that day, not by sweeping and mopping, but by sitting on one of the benches by the fireplace so that Miri could paint a picture of her. Teresa had always resisted getting paid to "sit," but now Miri was able to persuade her that that would be much more helpful than cleaning the floors.

She asked Teresa to make them some of the so-called coffee (really bitter chicory), which was a big treat for Teresa but actually disgusting to Miri who liked the real thing, Teresa boiled water on the coal-stove for it, then they settled down by the fireplace, Teresa gingerly sipped her coffee, afraid to make a move in case it would disturb Miri, and Miri, having set up her easel, swabbing away at a fresh canvas, feeling strangely inspired.

Miri painted for almost two hours, feeling quite enthusiastic about her progress. Teresa sat with dignity. When Miri announced that they were finished for the day, Teresa thanked her profusely, again and again. She never had a long rest like that. And to get paid for it!

Miri could not go into the village that evening. There would not be any mail delivery anyway, and she wanted to know whether Dantan was coming with Judy before she saw the crowd again, and could give them the news, if there were any. She would wait at the Hotel Palma Linda, in their airy spacious lobby, for Judy's call.

Miri took a bath at Hotel Palma Linda twice

a week. She was charged forty *pesetas* each time for all the hot water she wanted and for two big fluffy white towels. She would wait for Judy's call before starting her bath.

Some of the houses in the village also had their own hot water, provided from coal stoves, but Miri's had only cold water, which ran through the pipes only to the extent she could pump it herself.

Apart from a lack of creature comforts her house was magnificent – a hexahedron built of whitewashed concrete, situated dramatically on a remote hill, with a view of San Marino bay below. Across the bay could be seen small white buildings along the wharves, and a few tiny boats bouncing gently on the water.

One morning she had seen a rare rainbow; it arched across the sky, a full semi-circle.

Shepherds brought their sheep to graze on the scrub on her hill. Earlier in the year, when she first arrived, a shepherd had been leading a flock of tiny lambs. It could have been a scene out of the Old Testament. For all this she paid less than twenty dollars per month rent.

Judy's call, planned for six o'clock, came in at quarter-to-seven.

"It took forever to get through. What's so

urgent?" Judy asked excitedly. "Did Seymour come to visit you and you're getting married?"

Miri suppressed a sarcastic remark about Judy's line of thought. "No, something has happened here, and I think it would be very helpful if Alphie came down with you. A young local girl was found murdered, and the local police suspect a really nice decent local man who the foreigners think could not have possibly done it. In this country once you're arrested, that's it. You rot in jail. There's no due process to get you out, or even get you a fair trial. The only thing that will help Tomas is if someone can find the real murderer quickly. And I don't think any of the lushes and loungers here have the ability to do that." She told Judy the circumstances as she knew them. "If Alphie can somehow get involved in an investigation, Tomas may have a chance."

"If Alphie is willing to do it," Judy said doubtfully. "I think he was looking forward to getting rid of me for a little while," she giggled. "He was going to hack around Paris with Jean-Jacques and pretend he was a bachelor again. He has even started growing a moustache."

Yet again, Miri remarked to herself how shallow her friend was. How could growing a moustache be compared to solving a murder? "Well are you going to ask him?"

"Oh, of course. I think it would be great if he would agree. I just don't know...."

"I thought he would do anything you wanted."

"That was just in the beginning. He's still nice to me but he has his own ideas."

Miri couldn't help but think about Seymour. He had seemed so compliant, so eager to please her she had sort of taken him for granted. Until he got mad and broke off their relationship when she wouldn't accept his garnet ring. Maybe she could have handled the situation better.

"How late will you be at the Hotel Palma Linda? I could telephone you later, after Alphie has gotten home and I've had a chance to talk to him, or I could telephone you tomorrow evening, same time, same place, and let you know what Alphie said."

Miri hesitated only an instant, after calculating that she could afford to splurge on a meal at the hotel in order to pass the time awaiting Judy's call back. "I'll be here until you call. I'll have a big delicious meal here so they can find me when you call. I can always have my bath later."

"Great! Talk to you later."

When Dantan arrived home at eight-thirty

that evening, earlier than he had for weeks, he found his wife in a state of pleasurable excitement. They sat down to eat as soon as he had washed up. Germaine brought out the soup.

"Something very unusual has happened where Miri is living," Judy began enthusiastically.

If she had hoped to rouse his curiosity she failed. He was tucking into the excellent cold potato and leek soup, and was only half-listening.

Judy pouted. "Don't you want to know what it was?"

Dantan smiled. "I know you'll tell me."

"A young girl was found murdered there."

Dantan shrugged. In his line of work, this was not a remarkable event.

"There's no murder on Ibiza," Judy insisted. "This is very unusual. Not like Paris. Or," she added in the interest of fairness, "the States."

As he continued doggedly to spoon up his soup, and break off a crunchy piece of bread, Judy persisted. "The *Guardia Civil* are trying to arrest an innocent man. A local. As soon as they can catch up with him. Miri and all the expatriates there are sure he is innocent, and don't know what to do. Helping him get a lawyer wouldn't even be enough, they don't have real justice there. They're afraid that once he's found he'll be locked up and will rot in jail. Miri

thought you might be willing to come down there
with me and investigate."

Now Dantan sat up and took notice. His wife
was to have taken off shortly to visit her friend, and
he was rather looking forward to a bachelor's life
for a few days, going around the cafes with Jean-
Jacques Pilieu as they had done in the old days. "I
can't investigate a crime in Spain. I would have no
official standing, and would almost certainly not be
welcomed by the Spanish police into the investigation. I would not be able to view evidence, or con-
duct interrogations. I would have no access to re-
sources such as forensic technicians, or police find-
ings and interviews. Forget it. You go visit your friend,
and stay out of all that."

"Please, Alphie! You're so intelligent, you'll
think of something. And you don't have to tell anyone you're there to investigate the murder. After
all, you would just be going there socially, visiting
my friend Miri. You don't have to present yourself
in an official capacity, you'd just be a tourist. But
you'll meet all the foreigners who live there, and
I'm sure they will talk to you freely."

She got up from her seat opposite him and
went over and sat down in his lap, placing her arms
around him. "Anyway, I would like to have you with
me. We could have fun. You need a vacation after

that horrible Paginot case."

"I don't speak Spanish."

"All the foreigners speak English, and some of them speak Spanish too and could help out, plus there is a Frenchman there, and a French girl, a poetess. There's also a Belgian, I guess he speaks French too." Judy had been keeping up a gossipy correspondence with Miri, and appeared to know a lot about many of the expatriates there.

It was Judy's blandishments to be together that finally persuaded him. The faint urge to stray was dissipating. The idea of having his wife with him away "on a desert island" was appealing.

She thanked him with lavish hugs and kisses, and as soon as they finished the excellent *coq au vin* Germaine had provided, Judy proceeded to change her travel plans accordingly. "I'm going to call Miri right now and tell her. I know she'll be thrilled."

As Judy went to the living-room where the telephone was, Dantan called after her, "Tell Miri not to tell any of her acquaintances that a French police inspector is coming."

First, she called the Hotel Palma Linda to make sure she and Alphie would get a good room. That was no problem. There was a suite available, and it was one of the few accommodations to be equipped with an air-conditioner. Then she placed another call to the hotel, this one for Miri.

"Alphie will be coming with me," she announced happily. "As soon as I can get new airplane reservations, and know the date, I'll make a reservation at the Hotel Palma Linda. I've already talked to the hotel and there will be no problem getting a room. I'll send you a telegram with the details."

"You were going to stay at my house. You still can, with Alphie. My second bedroom has two beds."

"Since my husband is going to be along, I don't want to rough it." Unlike Miri's house, the Hotel Palma Linda had hot and cold running water, electricity, and an air-conditioner. "You won't have to pay a dollar for your baths," Judy giggled, "you can take one in our room whenever you want to."

"I'm really glad Alphie agreed."

"I almost forgot. Alphie said to tell you not to tell anyone that one of your visitors is a French police inspector."

"Why?"

"He didn't say. Maybe he doesn't want them to get their hopes up. Or maybe he doesn't want the *Guardia Civil* to hear, and get angry."

Miri could understand that, and agreed to keep quiet, although she had been bursting to relay the news as soon as Judy had told her Alphie agreed to come.

Back at her house, Miri felt a sudden impulse to write to Seymour, whose recent letter she had not yet answered. She lit the two kerosene lamps set on the table, found a piece of writing-paper and began: "Dear Seymour. Thank you for your letter. I bet you're happy to be getting out of the Army. Judy and Alphonse Dantan are coming down in a few days. Would you like to come too?" She made it clear that he was not invited to stay at her house. "There are some inexpensive *fondas* you could stay at. One in San Marino right in the village is *Fonda Bahia*. The owners are probably former Nazis but the food is good. Judy and Alphonse are going to stay at the most expensive hotel here, naturally."

Now that she had actually written a letter to Seymour, although she had procrastinated doing so, she was impatient to send it to him. Events on Ibiza moved slowly. The next outgoing mail would not be delivered to the next boat going to either Palma or Barcelona until the following evening, although of course it had to be mailed in the morning to be sure it was included in the evening packet.

The pace on Ibiza sometimes got on Miri's nerves. It was really only good for people who had nothing to do. The locals didn't seem to mind it, riding fifteen kilometers into town in their horse-drawn wagons, for three or four hours, or waiting for the rickety bus which only went in to town and back twice a day, and took more time than she could make it on her bicycle with the one-horsepower motor on the front wheel.

The locals didn't even seem to mind being poor as dirt, and working many hours each day in the sizzling sun for a few *pesetas*.

They seemed resigned to everything.

Some of the young people, however, were anxious to learn. Catalina had been taught English by her brother Tomas. But the illiterate maids and peasants tried pathetically to catch snatches from the foreigners. How come nobody protested? They were too resigned.

FOUR

LADY LUSH

Miri rode her Velo-Solex into the village quite early the next morning, eager to mail her letter to Seymour as soon as the post-office opened.

Very few of the foreigners had shown up yet at Liberto's. Only Harriet and Mavis were there, sipping *manzanilla.* They greeted Miri. They had been talking about Tomas. "He hasn't been seen at all, anywhere," said Harriet, "since he went to Ibiza in his truck."

"But I don't think he's guilty," Mavis said, "just that he doesn't want to be locked up." She reiterated her possible contribution. "As soon as I can get to see Vicente I'm going to ask him if he can hide Tomas in his boat or somewhere."

"If the *Guardia Civil* are still looking for him," Harriet said impatiently, "don't you think they would find him more easily in San Marino than in Ibiza city, which is more than five times bigger?"

"Maybe Nigel and the others have actually found him but of course don't want to give him away. He and Catalina have hordes of aunts and uncles and cousins, it would be easier for him to hide out with them."

"If only we could find proof of the real killer," Harriet sighed. "Then they would have to let up on Tomas. And we could all rest easier in our beds. You can be sure the maids at the *fonda* are quaking."

"Why? You think the killer is someone at the *fonda*?" Mavis asked, startled.

"I have no idea," said Harriet. "But it stands to reason that anyone at the *fonda*, a guest or an employee, had opportunity. Being a maid, Maria spent a lot of time at work. And we don't really know what went on behind the scenes at the boarding-house. There are men who work in the basement and kitchen that nobody ever sees. To say nothing of the *fonda* guests who are prime suspects."

"Prime suspects?"

"Well for one thing Jorgen is famous for wringing the necks of chickens!" Harriet said wryly. "I've heard of his exploits helping out in the *fonda* kitchen. Says he used to do it on the family farm back home in Sweden. And he's a big fellow. Nobody could hold their own against that giant, much less a frail little thing like Maria."

Miri was skeptical that Jorgen could be a killer; he was too good an artist. And furthermore, the time he had dropped in on her to see her paintings, he had been a perfect gentlemen. Unlike another surprise visitor she had had!

"Jorgen is an artist, not a killer." Miri said. "Who else do you suspect?"

"Well look at Max. We know he batters Francine...."

"Yes, and that's wrong, but she doesn't have to get back together with him, does she? And he hasn't killed her."

"Miri, anyone would think you had a soft spot for Max!" smiled Mavis.

"I don't. He's a boor. And nasty. But he is a writer, a real writer who writes."

Mavis said languidly, "You can't rule out someone because he's an artist."

Harriet agreed emphatically. "We can't rule out anyone with opportunity. Even Claude."

"Oh Claude's all right," said Mavis. "His worst fault is that he wants to open that abominable tourist-attraction restaurant. If there are any more murders around here, he might very well be the victim, not the killer, for trying to spoil our peace and quiet."

"And cheap prices," Harriet added.

"Even Hugo is not exempt, even though he looks like an oversized fat baby. After all, he lives at the *fonda* too."

"But why would any of these men do it?" Miri cried. "It makes no sense. If anyone at the *fonda* did it my vote is with Ilse. She's a mean bitch, treats her staff like dirt, and I could see her losing her temper and getting out of control. And they say she and her husband were Nazis during the war."

"She wouldn't kill off a hard-working underpaid maid like Maria," Mavis smiled. "No. We're no good as detectives. We'd better leave that to people like Nigel who seem to find out everything that is going on just by sitting around with a drink."

"If that's the way to solve the case then Liberto is the perfect detective," said Harriet. "I'm sure he knows more about any of us than we ourselves do. He's a perfect eavesdropper, with that fatuous smile of his."

"Friends of mine are coming from Paris for a short visit," Miri said encouragingly. "They will be staying at the Hotel Palma Linda."

"Painters like yourself?" Harriet asked.

"No," Miri blurted out, "my friend's husband is an inspector with the Paris *Police Judiciare*," too late recalling her promise not to reveal that bit of information.

"That's excellent!" exclaimed Harriet. "What is his name? Does he speak English? Spanish? You said 'friends' plural. Is he bringing an assistant?"

"He's coming with his wife, my friend. She's an American." Miri felt miserable that she had let the secret slip out. She hoped Dantan wouldn't be angry.

Telling Harriet and Mavis was like telling the entire expatriate community. Information travelled so swiftly it was almost as if they all participated in a group consciousness.

By the afternoon, when the diehard drinkers in the crowd would have gathered, that is, those that came to the village even when there was no mail delivery, everyone would know about the imminent arrival of a French detective, and would be pleasantly agitated at the thought of assisting in an investigation.

And of course Miri would get attention for bringing him. She would secretly like that even though she told herself that she didn't care that she wasn't popular with that crowd. They heartily concurred with Max's name for her, "Round Square".

But when Miri rode into the village later that afternoon, expecting the expatriates to bombard her with questions about the French inspector and his American wife who would be arriving on Thursday morning, there was nobody there except Max, who leered at her. She was uncertain about whether to sit down at the big cafe table or not when Max greeted someone behind her: "Lady Lush! What an honor!"

The regal blonde he was addressing, staggering but maintaining her dignity gave him a frosty look, then greeted Miri with a minimal smile. Liberto was instantly at her side with a cognac.

"Liberto! Round up all my countrymen as quickly as you can!"

"Yes, Lady Mary." And Liberto scurried off.

Miri rebuffed Max's next attempt at conversation, by looking around distractedly as if seeking the others. Not that any of them were really her friends.

Two small unpleasant young men, Edgar and Percy, whom Max had dubbed "Twit and Twerp," were the first to arrive, chattering shrilly. Lady Mary whispered something to them, and they were silenced, but sat on the edge of their chairs.

Miri had only met them twice previously, and both times they had raved on about their cats. Miri hated cats, and didn't particularly like cat owners either.

Nigel and Pamela arrived next, rubbing the long siesta from their eyes. Lady Mary patted a chair next to her, signalling Nigel to sit down. Pamela sat down on his other side.

Harriet then arrived, seating herself beside Pam. She seemed to have gotten wind that something unusual was up with the Brits, and was clearly trying to hear what was going on. Miri moved to sit down beside her.

Still Lady Mary gave no explanation.

Then the well-upholstered pair of "Saphists," Hazel and Dorcas, whom Miri rarely saw except on Thursdays trudging up the bumpy dirt road in their girdles and black dresses and shoes and stockings, to play bridge with Edgar and Percy, plumped down.

Seeing that the whole contingent was present, Lady Mary made her announcement. "My estate manager has informed me by telegraph that our man in London has been arrested and residing in a London jail."

A gasp arose from all. They all looked to be in a genteel panic.

Miri whispered to Harriet, "Who's their man in London?"

"Money-changer," Harriet whispered

brusquely. She clearly wanted to keep listening, not talk to Miri.

Nigel took over the discussion, beginning to propose steps they could take in this monetary crisis.

Miri was bewildered that the whole group apparently had one "money-changer" and why his arrest should cause such general panic. "Why can't they just go through a bank or something?"

Max explained. "Britain severely limits how much currency can be taken out of the country, no matter how rich you are. It apparently isn't much, not even for living in Ibiza if it's for a long stretch. The regulation limits someone as to where they can go, and for how long. However, some enterprising middle-European Jewish refugee came to their rescue. He developed a lucrative and mutually useful business, based on trust. An Englishman who wants to go abroad with more than the limited currency allowable on a monthly basis deposits pounds for the money-changer in London, and the money-changer in turn deposits an equivalent amount in the local currency where the Englishman is travelling. Naturally he charges a rich commission for this, so everyone is happy."

"Until he goes to jail," said Miri.

"Right," said Max, "now that their money-changer has been arrested, all the British here are worried about how to get *pesetas.*"

Harriet added, "While you two were babbling, they were trying to persuade Lady Mary to ask one of her servants to come out from England and smuggle in some emergency cash. But so far Lady Mary is resisting requesting a British servant to do anything illegal."

Harriet sad with an ironic smile, "Note that it's okay for a middle-European Jew to do so."

"I wish he hadn't been Jewish," Miri sighed.

"If he hadn't been Jewish he wouldn't have been a refugee," said Max.

Not a word had been spoken about the murder, or of Tomas. Everyone seemed to have lost interest in the subject very fast. Miri hesitated for a moment at the wisdom of inviting Alphie Dantan down to investigate if these people weren't going to take an interest. After all, their help would be needed if he was to get anywhere with the investigation. And why would he bother if they were not going to be interested?

"Any word about Tomas Bonet?" Miri ventured to ask.

As one, the Brits turned to look at her blankly.

Miri decided she would have to be glad to

see Dantan as well as Judy even if he didn't do any investigating.

The Dantans would be arriving on the boat from Mallorca on Thursday morning, two days away. Miri decided not to go into the village at all on Wednesday. Most of the crowd would be focussing on the jailed money-changer, not a visiting French detective, and this was her last chance to get some painting done before Judy arrived and would want to go shopping and seeking out expatriate artists' work for her collection. Miri planned on taking her to see Jorgen's sculpture, and would try to avoid Cindy's grasp for them to see Fred's work.

On Wednesday late morning, Miri clapped a big straw hat on her head, and trudged under the hot sun across the dusty baked fields to Teresa's cottage, to visit and to paint Teresa's bedridden daughter.

She had already done one painting of the little girl. Now the little girl's skin was even more yellow than the last time. The color made Miri very sad. She tried to capture it in the new painting she was working on, but there was something ominous about it.

Thursday morning, early, Miri took the rickety bus into Ibiza to meet the boat. The bus was full of fat chattering peasant women swathed in black, and thin haggard men also in black, mostly sitting silent. Miri thought of doing a painting of them, but it would have cost her too much in bus fares going back and forth enough times to get the sketches. To say nothing of the airless discomfort of the bus. She did make a few sketches in the small notebook she kept with her.

Miri sat at a dockside cafe sipping black coffee, along with other locals and foreigners awaiting the slow chugging of the boat into its berth. The gangplank was lowered, the porters began bringing down luggage and suddenly there was a rush of passengers debarking. Miri spotted Dantan and Judy, rumpled from travel but still fashionable. As it happened they couldn't get berths and had had to sleep on deck all night, romantic under the stars except for those passengers also in deck-chairs who occasionally threw up, not always making it to the railing.

After hugging and exclaiming over how well each looked, Miri wanted to take them to a cafe for a breakfast probably better than the scant rolls and coffee they could get on board. Dantan would have agreed, but his wife was itching to get to her nice air-conditioned room in San Marino and take a bath first. It was an easy matter to locate a taxi, one of the few old beat-up black vehicles in sight, and they rumbled off to San Marino, Judy keeping up a constant line of patter about the sights: black-clad farmers in slow-moving horse-drawn wagons, black-swathed peasant women bending over in the fields, an occasional lithe tan dog running rampant. Miri had long since stopped considering all this picturesque. It was too hot.

FIVE

A BRIEFING AT BREAKFAST

While Judy carefully unpacked her tissue-wrapped dresses (and all the other items she had deemed it necessary to bring), carefully hung up her dresses and Alphie's jacket and slacks, stashed the underwear, swimming things, and a variety of shoes and slippers, and undertook to repair a seemingly perfect manicure, Dantan sat quietly on the rattan sofa, next to a table still piled high with a sumptuous breakfast the hotel had provided for the Dantans on their arrival.

Miri, amazed by her friend's color-coordinated wardrobe, was also silent.

It was Judy broke the silence. "Miri, what is there to do in this place evenings?" She sounded as if she expected her friend to say, "Nothing."

"Apart from sitting in a cafe and gossiping about the foreigners that are absent....Well, there's the peasant dances. All the tourists go to see them at least once. They wear elaborate colorful costumes and the dancing is odd. The men skitter around the women. Like cocks around hens according to some English people who know barnyard animals. You just missed the big festival, of course, the one I wrote you about, to celebrate throwing out the Moors in some old century or other."

"Sounds thrilling. What else?"

"The Sunday movie. Everybody goes. It's shown in a fenced-in field and the picture is projected against the wall of a whitewashed stone barn. Folding-chairs are set up right on the ground. They always show an American Western or jungle adventure, dubbed in Spanish. Not only is the dubbing unintelligible, but the censors have mutilated the dialogue so that even if you can understand the Spanish, the story makes no sense. You just have to enjoy looking at Charlton Heston or someone like that. The locals comment freely and loudly throughout the show and cheer the good guys. Some people buy a big bar of sickenly sweet Spanish chocolate. I do. Last Sunday, they showed a football tear-jerker with a really good-looking actor, Ronald Reagan, in a bit part. But since I don't know anything about football, and don't want to, I didn't try to follow the dubbing. The crowd went nuts."

"It's a tough decision between that and the chickens dancing," Dantan said drily.

"There's also the *paseo* on Sunday, the unmarried girls slowly walking around the plaza, wearing all their beads and jewelry at once, and the boys gaping at them. Anyway, dinner starts so late and lasts so long you won't need any other entertainment, you'll be too sleepy by that time."

"I'm glad I want to shop for native stuff," giggled Judy, "And see you, of course, because otherwise this isn't the liveliest place I could think of!"

"The swimming is delicious, as long as you don't step on any conches. And you'll have fun shopping, the prices are so unbelievably low." Miri wiggled her foot, on which was a black canvas sandal with a straw sole. "Two dollars."

"I like my Italian leather sandals better. And I have seven pairs of them. All different colors. To match my new dresses."

"You'll wear them out in no time on these rough roads. Better buy some *alpargatas* for while you're here."

"I would like to ask Miri," Dantan put in a little restively, "to tell me what she knows about what happened."

"Please start from the beginning," Judy pleaded. "I don't want to miss a thing."

Dantan nodded at Miri and smiled. He had already started making notes with his "bic" in the new notebook he had bought for "the case."

"I told you. Early Monday morning, a young man, Tomas Bonet, whose father owns a successful general-store in town, found the body of a young girl beside his truck parked at the docks. He didn't know she was dead, he thought she was just unconscious, so he drove her to the doctor, and when the doctor wouldn't see her right away, left to go on his errands in town. Tomas' sister Catalina told us this as we were all having breakfast at Liberto's cafe. She was all upset, because the *Guardia Civil* were looking for Tomas because the doctor said the girl was already dead. Catalina was terrified that Tomas would get arrested and imprisoned and never come out. It can happen like that in Spain."

"Did Catalina say how Tomas thought the girl's body got there, beside his truck?" To Dantan the simplest explanation was that Tomas had killed her himself.

"She didn't say. And of course nobody in the crowd got to speak with Tomas himself. Nobody knows where he is. Of course, Catalina might, but she's not telling. Monday morning, as soon as Catalina told us what had happened, Jorgen and Nigel and Pamela took a taxi to Ibiza city with her to warn Tomas that the police wanted to arrest him, and he hasn't been back to San Marino since."

"So according to Catalina, after Tomas, the doctor was the next person to see the body?"

"The doctor's maid. She opened the door for him, but refused to call the doctor right away, because it was too early. She had been ordered not to disturb him while he was still sleeping. He always left strict instructions not to be disturbed until he came downstairs to his office."

"But it might be an emergency."

But the maid repeated that she was not supposed to disturb the doctor until he came downstairs to his office.

"That doesn't sound consistent with the Hippocratic Oath," Dantan said sarcastically. "What did Tomas do then?"

"He placed the girl in a big chair in the doctor's hallway, told the assistant to tell the doctor to look at her as soon as possible, and then left. He said that he didn't know she was dead."

"Do you know if any of your crowd has managed to speak with the doctor?"

"I don't know anything about that. But there's

a sort of ringleader of the expatriates, the one who likes to take charge, a middle-aged Englishman named Nigel, so he would be the one to ask. If anyone knows, he would. He has a girlfriend, Pamela, also English. She's plump and smiles a lot to show off her dimples. Max calls her "Dumples." He's given everyone nicknames."

"What's yours?" Judy giggled. She had been listening quietly while eating steadily.

"They don't call me it to my face, but this busybody from the Midwest, Harriet, told me. "It's 'Round Square'."

"What's that supposed to mean?"

"Never mind."

Dantan asked Miri, "Do you think one of the expatriates could have done it?"

"Why would any of them? But I don't think it was Tomas either. He's too nice. Maybe it was one of the fishermen who dock their boats at the wharf."

Dantan thought this might be worth looking into. "What else is around there?"

"A couple of bars or restaurants, I think. Not much."

"How can all these foreigners afford to just live here indefinitely?" Judy asked.

"Well, if you have any money at all it's very cheap, as you can see. On what I saved while working in Paris, I can live here for at least ten months, longer if I'm really careful. You two are staying at the most luxurious place in San Marino, but people can live here for a month for what one night in your suite costs. A lot of the British, especially, have incomes from their capital. Even if it's small, it goes far."

"Are there many British here?"

"Besides Nigel and Pamela, there is actually a member of the British nobility, or is it aristocracy? I get those two mixed up. Lady Mary, a gracious pleasant drunk. Max has named her 'Lady Lush'. She almost never shows up in the mornings, too busy sleeping off the night before, but she sometimes comes to the evening gathering. Just about everyone does on evenings when a boat has called at Ibiza – around every other day – because that's when the mail is available at the post-office. Letters come by boat in the morning, then the postal people sort them, and when the post-office reopens around six in the afternoon you can pick up your mail. Theoretically, they open at five, but they never do until around six.

"Then there is a pair of middle-aged British women, Max calls them 'The Saphists,' Dorcas and Hazel, who keep house together. Hazel is round and nice and does their cooking and gardening, Dorcas is tough and does the carrying and fixing. They always wear tight corsets and black dresses and stockings and heels when they visit their English friends. They keep a pink-nosed Ibicencan hound as a pet. They've named her Mabel. All Mabel's cohorts roam free and wild and don't appear to have specific owners. But Mabel seems to stay with them.

"Then there are two thin small unfriendly Englishmen, Edgar and Percy, who hardly ever hang out with the crowd. They keep house together, and have three cats. Percy writes reviews of unknown books for unknown journals. Max has named them 'Twit and Twerp.' I never can remember which is which.

"The English crowd are mostly oddballs. Nigel is okay, but he just hangs around all the time, never does anything. Doesn't even *pretend* to write or paint or anything. In fact, I can't think of any of the English who do any *work*. Unless you call trying to grow roses in hot sun, sand, and no rain, work. Hazel does that."

This was all very interesting to his wife, but Dantan felt they were getting off track. If he truly was to be of some help in the matter of the murder, he wanted as much information as he could get. From Miri, for starters. "Tell me what you know about the dead girl," he asked.

"Her name is Maria Figuera. She was fourteen years old. An Ibizan. She worked as a housemaid at the *Fonda Bahia* in the village. Her sister Consuelo, who's a year or two older, works in the kitchen there. Now that Maria is dead, I heard that Consuelo is also doing housework at the *fonda* besides her own work in the kitchen. Maria also did cleaning for some of the foreigners."

"Do you know who, specifically, she worked for?"

Miri shook her head. "No, but I might be able to find out from the woman who works for me, Teresa. Teresa mostly works in the fields, to be nearer her sick daughter, but she also cleans for a few people – I'm one of them – and she works at the *fonda* on Sunday nights so that the younger girls can get off to go to the *paseo*. None of them make very much money. I pay Teresa four *pesetas* an hour – that's a dime – and one of the owners of the *fonda*, Ilse, used to pay Teresa three *pesetas*, so she got angry at me for causing inflation. Now all the maids get four *pesetas* from the foreigners, and Ilse also had to up them from three. Two-and-a-half cents difference.

"That's why a lot of them can't go anywhere, even to Barcelona. But I never heard anyone com-

plain. Not even Teresa, whose daughter is bedridden with nobody knows what. I wish I could afford
to take her and her daughter to a doctor in Barcelona,
but I'm too selfish, I want my money for living here
and painting."

"That's not selfish," Judy said, "people do
take care of themselves first. Unless you're a saint,
of course, and luckily you're not even Catholic," she
giggled, "so you don't have to worry about being a
saint."

Dantan, who had been born and baptised
Catholic but now practiced no religion, was amused
to hear that his wife had known even this much
about his former religion. One of these days they
would be having children, he hoped, and it seemed
evident his father-in-law would be adamant that the
children be raised as Jews. He himself preferred to
finesse the subject and teach the children, when they
were old enough to understand, Bible stories as if
they were just another group of fairy tales he would
be reading them, along with Hans Christian
Andersen and The Brothers Grimm. But he and Judy
had not yet discussed it.

"When will you be able to see Teresa?" he
asked Miri.

"She works at my house on Mondays."

"Besides the maids, who else works at the

fonda?"

"The coal-stoker, who is also general handy-
man. The *fonda* has running hot water. But I don't
know much about the place. You could ask one of
the expatriates who lives there. There's Claude, a
very nice Frenchman I'm sure you will enjoy meeting. And Hugo, the Belgian, Flemish to be specific,
a fat gross liar nobody likes. Max has named him
'The Belch.' And Jorgen, a gigantic Swede, Max calls
him the 'Great Dane,' who makes sculptures out of
stones he finds in the fields. He's very strong and
always lugging around his stones in a sack. Oh, and
Francine, a young French poetess. She was living
with Max, who is a brute, but then she moved out
of his house, probably because he gave her one black
eye too many. She says it was because she couldn't
get enough poetry written when he was around.
Then there are always tourists, coming and going.
Nobody bothers getting to know them, they don't
stay long enough. Fred, the American artist who
paints like Jackson Pollock, would like to – the females, that is – but his wife Cindy keeps him on a
really short leash."

"Did Maria ever work for Max?"

"I don't know. I could ask Francine. If Max
lets me. He hates when Francine talks to anyone
else, male or female. Probably because a lot of

people would try to urge her to drop Max. Anyway, Francine is not always around. She hides out when her bruises show too much."

"How awful!" said Judy. "Why does she associate with him at all?"

"If there were no masochists there could be no sadists," Dantan said.

"I told you these people were oddballs," Miri said to Judy.

"What about this busybody from the Midwest, Harriet?" Dantan asked. A busybody could be a very useful source of information.

"She likes everybody, even The Belch, and she's very good at worming personal information out of people. Except me. I've managed not to tell her the private things on my mind."

"What's that?" Judy inquired.

"If I told you, then it wouldn't be private anymore."

"Is it about Seymour?"

"It would be extremely useful to question the doctor," Dantan said, following his own trend of thought. "Do any of the foreigners know him?"

"As far as I know, only Cindy, Fred's wife, and she has nothing but contempt for him. Understandably. He nearly killed her. She went to him with a female complaint and he wanted to remove her appendix. She eventually had to go to Barcelona to find a competent doctor. Everyone knows of a local boy who died at his hands, having his appendix removed. Rumor is that the doctor used unclean implements. And who knows if it was even a case of appendicitis? That might be the only thing the doctor knows how to do!"

"Why would anyone go to him?"

"It took awhile for word about his incompetence to get around the expatriates, and as far as the peasants, most of them can't afford to go further afield. Just going to Ibiza city is a big deal, much less to Palma or Barcelona."

"Is there anyone else I should know about?"

"Fred and Cindy, and Max, and Harriet, and me, we're the only Americans. There was a young couple here for awhile but they've gone off to India or someplace like that to study Far Eastern philosophies. The Germans are Hans and Ilse, they own the *Fonda Bahia*, and there's a German Jewish couple, Lotte and Leo, both painters. They have concentration-camp tattoos on their arms. They live in a remote peasant's house in the fields. Claude and Francine are the only French here, except the few tourists who breeze through."

"If I am to get to talk with any of the Ibizans, I'll need someone I can trust who will be able to translate for me."

"It depends whether the particular Ibizan speaks Spanish or not. Some of them don't. The really illiterate ones only speak Ibicencan. That is unintelligible, even if you know Spanish. It's a dialect of Catalan. But even if someone could understand Catalan, I'm not sure they could understand Ibicencan. Mavis is trying to learn it, so as to be able to talk with her lover Vicente, but I don't think she's gotten very far. Their communications seem mostly physical.

"The one foreigner who might be able to help is Claude. His Spanish is fluent, but not only that, he's trying to learn Ibicencan because he's thinking of starting a business here. Of course, there's Tomas and Catalina, who speak English, Spanish and Ibicencan...."

Dantan would try to meet Nigel and Claude as soon as possible, to get started.

"And Mavis might be helpful, as her lover is Ibicencan and knows the locals."

"I'm not going to want any lunch," Judy announced, patting her tummy.

"I'm going back to my house now," Miri said.

Judy motioned for Miri to wait, and produced a small gift-wrapped package from her make-up case. "It's Noxyema," she said. "Slather it on when-ever you go out. If you spend much time in this hot sun your skin will start to look like my Aunt Mildred's who spends every winter in Miami. Her face looks like an old shoe."

Miri unscrewed the jar's lid. "Ugh! What a smell! Are you two going to take a *siesta*?"

Judy yawned and looked at Alphie who smiled.

"Want to meet in the village around five-thirty?" Miri asked. "You'll have time to go for a swim after your *siesta*, and later you can meet as many of the expatriates as show up for the mail and the evening drinking. They start showing up around five, sometimes earlier."

"I may walk in earlier," Dantan told his wife. "But Madame here can come whenever she wishes."

"I'll be there at five or five-thirty or so," Judy giggled. "I want to meet all the oddballs."

Miri gave them strict instructions that if they went swimming they were to look out for conches, which clung to the slippery rocks in the water at al-most every spot along the beach. "They're like little round porcupines and if you step on one it will hurt like hell and lots of the needles will stick in your foot and they have to be taken out one by one."

"I'm not going to swim," Judy said. "Just relax under an umbrella."

Miri trudged back to her house under an intense sun. She wondered, who would have killed a harmless child? She couldn't imagine anyone she knew doing such a thing. The peasants and the fishermen and the local merchants seemed very nice. Far nicer than she herself would have been had she had to live such a miserable life.

Max? He had hurt Francine numerous times. But not fatally. He punched and slapped her around. But she hadn't stopped seeing him.

Could Tomas have actually done it after all? Suppose he had grabbed Maria the way he had grabbed Miri that time, and the young girl had resisted and threatened to tell on him.

Or had Maria seen something she shouldn't have? But what could that possibly be? The expatriates in San Marino might be odd, but they weren't bad.

It was a puzzle. She hoped Dantan could figure it out. She would hate for it to be Tomas after all.

When she got home she didn't feel like painting. She had eaten too much. When she didn't feel like painting she was miserable. For one thing, that was the sole reason she had come to this hot and arid place. For another, there was nothing much else to do. She could go for a swim, but that wouldn't take long.

She could read a book, but she had read all the books she had brought with her and had found them boring. And there was no place in San Marino to buy new ones. Teresa sometimes found books at the *fonda* that a tourist had thrown out before leaving but usually she gave them to Consuelo Figuera, who was desperately trying to learn English. Consuelo had never been to school. Neither had most of the peasant girls. Miri thought maybe she should splurge on a trip to Mallorca and buy a few books in Palma. She was getting short on Cadmium White anyway. Or maybe even Barcelona! Then she could go see the Gaudis that Cindy and Fred had told her about. But a trip to Barcelona, with the boat, and a place to stay, might cost her two weeks here in San Marino. Two weeks less to try to paint.

SIX

MORE QUESTIONS

Dantan had no illusions that he would be able to distance himself from the expatriates who had already been primed to expect magic from him. Besides, he rather liked having something to think about. He loved his wife, but he was more completely happy when he was working.

He began to note down some basic questions:

Motive: The victim was poor, uneducated, hard-working, and fourteen years old. Who would want to kill her?

Opportunity: who had access to her?

Circumstances: Where did the murder occur? When did the murder occur? How was she killed?

At this point Dantan had few facts that would suggest answers to any of these questions.

Maria had worked at the *Fonda Bahia* as a maid. But she had also sometimes cleaned for one or more of the foreigners who had their own houses. She lived in a small house in the village with her mother and sister Consuelo, who also worked at the *fonda.* On Sundays, she went to Mass, walked the *paseo* with the other young unmarried girls, and sometimes attended the movie in the field held on Sunday nights. She did not go to school. The only shopping she did was for food or coal. She never went anywhere outside San Marino.

The circles of people she came into contact with could be clearly defined: her mother and sister, their neighbors, other girls her age; the priest; the owners of the *fonda,* Ilse and Hans; the *fonda* employees -- the coal-stoker, the cook, the laundresses. Then there were the guests of the *fonda*: tourists, of course, arrived and departed. The longer-term residents included Francine, a French poetess; Claude, a recent arrival interested in doing business in San Marino; Hugo, a typical expatriate simply spending his time in self-indulgence; Jorgen, the Swedish sculptor, who lived at the *fonda* and worked at his sculpture in its basement.

Dantan would want to find out for which foreigners Maria cleaned house. Miri might learn something from her own maid on Monday. And Maria's sister Consuelo could be expected to know.

Why would any one of these people want to kill the girl? Did she overhear something that would incriminate someone? If this was the case, then the murderer would have to be an Ibizan, for Maria spoke only Ibicencan, not even Spanish, and would not have understood anything in any other language.

Of course, if it was something she saw, then everyone was suspect; language would not be an issue.

Had she enraged someone? If so, what could have been significant enough to incite murder? Suppose a man had made unwanted advances to her, and she had not only resisted, but threatened to tell someone in authority, the priest, or the police, or her mother.

Could it have been a tragic accident in the course of some sexual game? This was highly unlikely considering the mores of the island. But human instincts were the same everywhere.

Was she caught stealing? Theft was usually not a motive for murder, but there were two people who might react with fury if their business was threatened: the owners of the *Fonda Bahia*, Hans and Ilse.

Where had the murder occurred? Well, the body was said to have been found beside Tomas

Bonet's truck. This had not yet been established as a fact. At this point it was hear-say: Miri said that Tomas' sister Catalina had said that Tomas had said that that was where he found it.

Assuming that the body had, in fact, been found beside Tomas' truck, that did not answer the question, Where had the murder been committed? Perhaps right there, where the body was found. But perhaps somewhere else, and the body transported to the docks.

If the murder had occurred elsewhere and the body transported to the truck, why? One obvious answer was that the killer did not want the body found anywhere in his vicinity. But why leave it near Tomas' truck? Perhaps to incriminate him?

When had the murder occurred? So far, all he knew was that Catalina had reported the event to the expatriates as they were imbibing their morning beverages at Liberto's cafe. Dantan could estimate the earliest time only after learning when she had last been seen alive.

How was she killed? Dantan would have to talk to someone who had seen or examined the body. There was always the remote possibility that she had died a natural death.

By the time Judy had finished unpacking and taken her long-anticipated bath, and Dantan had completed, for the moment, his initial notes on the case, it was time for lunch.

The spread at the Hotel Palma Linda dining-room was tempting, but Judy (in a sleeveless yellow linen sheath and matching yellow sandals) and Dantan ate sparingly, still feeling the effects of the sumptuous breakfast. Judy looked around to see if there were any guests she might want to get to know, but there were only a few patrons, stout men with black moustaches, wearing white suits.

Dantan had plans other than sleep for their after-lunch *siesta*. Back in their suite, he turned the bedroom air-conditioner up as high as possible and thought to check the filter, which, he saw, was coated with a thick layer of fuzz. With that cleaned that off, the room became cool enough for making love.

Afterwards, Judy drifted into a sound sleep. Dantan did not disturb her. He changed into swim-trunks and went down to the beach for a swim by himself. The water was pristine, sparkling and cool. He gave proper deference to the rocks in the shallow water and the conches clinging to them, and enjoyed himself very much. When he returned to their room Judy was still sleeping. He wrote her a note, saying he was walking into the village and would be there whenever she decided to show up.

Exchanging his beach shoes for hiking boots,

and swimsuit for rough shorts, he clapped the old tennis hat on his head that Judy had thought to pack, and walked through the large pleasant lobby to the dirt road outside. He trudged the two kilometers to the village. The sun was dazzling, and very hot.

He passed no people, animals or vehicles on his walk.

Liberto's cafe dominated San Marino's small plaza near the water. Two men were sitting together to one side of a large table shaded by an old Cinzano umbrella. One, in his forties, was fair-haired, had a paunch, and was surprisingly pale. The other, younger, was a powerfully built giant with red hair, a red beard, and a face deeply bronzed by the sun.

The young waiter skittered up to Dantan and grinned, "*Señor* English?"

The middle-aged one signalled the waiter to seat the newcomer with them. "Nigel," he said pleasantly to Dantan.

Aha, here is the Englishman Miri had said was the ringleader of the expatriate colony, thought Dantan. The giant stood up and thrust his hand forward to shake hands with Dantan. "Jorgen," he smiled, with a bone-crushing handshake. "*God dag.*"

"Alphonse Dantan," Dantan responded. "My wife and I are visiting a friend of hers, Miri Winter."

"We've all been looking forward to your arrival, Inspector," said Nigel.

"Thank you. Please drop the 'Inspector', just call me 'Dantan'," he said as he joined them at their table.

"Understood. Your title should not be bruited about."

A little late for discretion, Dantan thought wryly, with Liberto hovering very nearby, awaiting his order. If he hadn't already known who Dantan was (and Dantan doubted that there was little that escaped this bright-eyed alert young man), he surely knew it now.

He would have to make a point of questioning Liberto himself, once he felt he had won the young man's trust.

Dantan ordered a cognac. Nigel and Jorgen were drinking the same.

Nigel said, "We've been awaiting you eagerly, Dantan. We're hoping you can avert a miscarriage of justice."

Dantan said, "Naturally I'll do what I can to help, but I must tell you I do not intend to be assertive in any criminal investigation. The local police have not invited me to join any investigation, and I believe they would be justifiably perturbed if I injected myself unofficially. I am here with my wife Judy on vacation, to visit her friend Miri and

sightsee. I'll do what I can to help but only whatever I am able to do discreetly and without interfer-
ing with the police investigation."

"We understand all that," Nigel said impatiently, "but your professional powers of observa-
tion and deduction may lead to important information. You can do a lot, as a foreigner and a tourist,
accepted into the bosom of the expatriate colony.
We are all prepared to cooperate. Furthermore, the
local police seem to have halted any further search
for any suspects, in view of their *a priori* judgment
that Tomas Bonet is the culprit."

At that moment, Jorgen left a few coins on
the table, stood up with a nod to Nigel and Dantan,
and strode off.

"Too bad he left so abruptly," Dantan remarked. He was going to want to talk with Jorgen,
who lived and worked at the *fonda* where the murdered girl had worked. He had noted Jorgen's powerful muscles, and Miri had said Jorgen was often
seen hauling huge rocks from the fields for his sculpture. He was certainly capable of carrying the body
of a frail young girl. It would be hard for that giant,
however, to avoid being noticed.

"The 'Great Dane', as Max calls him, even
though he is Swedish, likes his nip, but he doesn't
linger much. He is, in fact, dedicated to his work."

Nigel sounded as if this were slightly incomprehensible to him. "He spends considerable time at it. I'm sure you'll get many opportunities to talk with him."

Dantan nodded. He said, "I'd like to begin by seeing where the body was discovered. I was told that her body was found by the side of a truck. Tomas Bonet's. And I'd like to see the truck...."

"I can show you where it was parked when Tomas found her body, but we don't know where the truck is just now. Tomas drove off Monday morning and neither he nor his truck has been seen since. The most likely place for him to have gone was Ibiza city, but Jorgen, Pam and I rode into town with his sister Catalina, and walked around quite a bit looking for it and couldn't find it. Or him."

"And he hasn't been seen since?"

"No. At least not by anyone willing to say so."

"Fleeing may of course imply guilt."

"Not in Spain. You would flee, too, if you knew the conditions a prisoner is subjected to here. As you may have heard, there is no such principle that a man is innocent until proven guilty. He's guilty if the police say he is."

"Well, I would still find it helpful to see the area where the girl was found. Try to assess whether anyone could have seen anything."

"Care to go there now? It's just a short walk along the docks."

Past Liberto's cafe was another waterside cafe with a few customers, then a bare stretch. Not much farther along a small cluster of fishing-boats bobbed gently in the water, and opposite the wharf, a restaurant – empty of guests. Next was a dark bar where a few old men stood at a counter, and then a small shop empty of customers but crammed with nets, baskets, anchors and other fishermen's gear. Not exactly a bustling part of town.

"We've actually overshot our mark," Nigel said. "I wanted you to see the nearest signs of life. The place where Tomas always parked his truck is actually about thirty meters before this spot." Empty space faced the spot. The shops and restaurants did not extend this far.

The two men retraced their steps. Dantan examined the ground, but could find no telling marks, no tire-tracks, no blood stains.... "How do you know this is the spot?"

"It's just a guess, of course, but everyone was used to seeing Tomas' truck here whenever he wasn't driving it."

Dantan indicated the restaurant, bar and shop. "Can you line up an interpreter for me? Or perhaps you could do it yourself? I'd like to talk with each of the proprietors and their employes."

"I'm afraid I'd be inadequate to the task," Nigel said apologetically. "Although my Spanish is a cut above rudimentary, many of the locals are ignorant of Spanish, and speak only their Ibicencan dialect. We need someone with English and Spanish and Ibicencan, at best, or, if no English, I could struggle along in my Spanish and have the other one translate into Ibicencan."

"Do you know anyone like that?"

"Only Catalina and, of course her brother Tomas, that I know of. Oh, and Liberto. Asking Catalina, involved as she is, would not be the most desirable. An Australian woman in our midst, Mavis, is very close with one of the local fishermen. But I believe they communicate by extrasensory perception, since Vicente speaks only Ibicencan, no Spanish, and Mavis no Ibicencan. Even her Spanish is rudimentary. The murder of a local girl, of course, has all the village abuzz. Vicente somehow managed to communicate to Mavis that he learned that the police have stored the body in the butcher's icehouse. Vicente has already arranged with the butcher to get you into the ice-house to view the body. This can be done very discreetly."

"Good. That could be helpful. I've already heard that Tomas took the body to the doctor, thinking she was merely unconscious. I wonder how much information I can get out of the doctor?"

"Just getting to talk with him is a long shot. He's not a popular figure around here."

"How do you know the girl was killed? Maybe she died of natural causes."

"In the opinion of the *Guardia Civil* she was murdered, and they were looking for the man they had made up their minds had killed her."

Dantan would need more proof than that. He didn't trust the medical acumen of policemen assigned to an extreme backwater where nothing ever happened.

Back at Liberto's cafe the two men had just sat down when they were joined by a burly black bearded man of medium height and considerable breadth. He grinned devilishly at Dantan. "Inspector Dupin, I presume?"

Dantan smiled back. "I take that as a compliment."

Nigel, who apparently had not heard of Inspector Dupin, looked from one to the other, nonplussed.

Dantan and Max shook hands. Max had a firm but not bone-crushing grip.

Liberto placed a cognac before Max without his having been asked.

"We all have been looking for you eagerly. Most of this crowd have their bowels in an uproar over what they have assured themselves is a miscarriage of justice, or will be, once Tomas Bonet is picked up," Max said. "In my opinion, Tomas Bonet is the most likely suspect. Occam's razor."

Dantan could see Max' point of view. Tomas had found the body, and it had been lying on the ground beside his own truck. But of course if Max had had anything to do with the murder, it would certainly be in his interest to divert suspicion to someone else!

"Other than that it would be the simplest explanation, do you have any other ideas or evidence to support it?"

"None. I don't even know when the murder occurred."

"Yes, that will be a very important fact to ascertain."

"The body was found early Monday morning," Nigel said, "when Tomas went to his truck, but it could have been placed there Sunday night, for all anyone knows."

"And what were you doing Sunday night?" Dantan smiled at Max.

"Effing my girl."

"All evening?"

"We didn't leave the house," Max said gruffly. "Well, Dupin, let me know if there is anything I can do to help, although I doubt it."

"Thank you. Do you recall when was the last time you saw Maria?"

Max looked startled, perhaps at actually being questioned. "I don't recall. Sometime last week. She cleaned my house late in the week. But she was certainly alive long after that."

Liberto brought Max a second cognac without asking. Max quaffed it in one gulp, then got up and said "so long."

Dantan would like to know what else Max might know. After Max left, Dantan asked Nigel, "Was it my simple questions that drove him off?"

"I very much doubt it. Max is sufficiently impervious to slurs or innuendos and can handle a lot more pressure than that! But he may be in the middle of writing something. He actually makes money at writing. He made enough money on his last book, a spy adventure, to pay for the house he is building here."

"He's going to settle here?" Dantan was surprised. He had sized Max up as a wanderer.

"I very much doubt that. He'll build something smashing, then sell out when the market goes up, and take off for Tahiti or Madeira."

"Do you think the market will go up?"

"There are some dangerous early warnings. There's talk that the Hotel Palma Linda is planning to build a big swimming pool despite the fact that they have one of the prettiest natural beaches in San Marino. And earlier this year a royal couple on their honeymoon anchored their yacht in our bay for a few days. That event was written up in the English press. And then there is the Frenchman, Claude – " he smiled at Dantan " – the *other* Frenchman here keeps talking about what a great tourist attraction an *haute cuisine* French restaurant would be, and he is seriously considering establishing one. Those of us who live here cheaply and quietly don't *want* San Marino to become a tourist attraction. Yes, I'm afraid Pam and I will be looking for another place to roost one of these days. Perhaps the Canary Islands .... And so would a number of the others."

"It would be helpful to question the other *fonda* guests about their activities Sunday night, as well as the *fonda* staff."

"Jorgen has already had his nip and will be working in his studio until dark. But Claude and the Belge should be showing up here eventually. As for the staff, that will have to be set up discreetly, through one of the locals. If Ilse gets wind she'll be furious. Anything that would cast suspicions on her establishment, don't you know."

"Now for Claude and Hugo?"

"Right. We just sit at Liberto's and wait."

But neither Claude nor the Belge had appeared by the time Dantan got tired of waiting around. Seeing them a day later wouldn't make any difference. The others who had arrived – Harriet, Mavis, and Lotte and Leo – stared intensely at Dantan. He made no effort to speak with them just yet.

"I heard there were numerous Englishmen in San Marino," Dantan said conversationally to Nigel.

"I'm afraid you'll have to wait a bit to meet my compatriots," Nigel said with a nervous laugh. "We're having a bit of a problem getting money out of England at the moment and my friends are revisiting the problem *ad nauseum.*"

Nigel himself appeared nonchalant on this subject. He seemed to believe that the problem would be resolved without his having to get much involved. Or perhaps he and Pamela had something put by here to last them through such crises.

"I'll be around awhile," Dantan assured him.

Liberto scurried over to see if either of them wanted another drink. Nigel assented, Dantan said he wanted to get back to his wife. He asked Liberto,

"Young man, what do think about what has happened?"

Liberto looked stunned. "What do I think?"

"Yes. What do you think?"

"I don't know what I think. Nobody has ever asked me before what I think."

"Well think about it then, and tell me another time."

Liberto broke into a broad smile. "*Si, Señor* English."

"French. I'm French. You may as well get that right."

Liberto nodded vigorously. "*Si, Señor* French."

SEVEN

LIBERTO'S AGAIN

The next day, after a late and substantial breakfast, Dantan and Judy took a taxi into the village. There was a large crowd sitting, jammed against one another, at Liberto's biggest table. Miri was already there, her Velo-Solex leaning against her usual palm tree, near Hugo's Vespa.

As Judy stepped out of the taxi, all heads turned to inspect her. The men looked appreciatively. Judy's buxom and curvaceous form in her chic sleeveless beige linen sheath and matching sandals looked very fetching. The women took fresh appraising looks at Dantan, his wiry vigorous body in slim black slacks and black Italian sports shirt, his pencil-thin black moustache, and his intelligent brown eyes.

Cindy glanced angrily at her husband when she noticed that Fred was gazing with open admiration and lust at Judy Dantan.

Miri made introductions and Judy began chatting like old friends with the women. Cindy kept a watchful eye on her but said little until she overheard Judy mention her budding art collection. Then she injected some promotional remarks about her husband's work.

"I heard you'd arrived," Fred grinned at Dantan, "otherwise I'd be splattering away in my studio." Fred was movie-star good-looking but soft, with long brown eyelashes like a woman's. His wife was short and taut, with short auburn curly hair.

"We're not going to hang around long," Cindy said sternly, "but we came because we wanted to help in any way you think we can."

Dantan thanked them both. He asked them when was the last time they had seen Maria.

"We have not seen Maria at all," Cindy answered for both of them. Fred nodded his assent.

Claude and Nigel were also looking at Judy admiringly. Only after everyone, it seemed, had sized up the curvaceous and fashionable wife of the French detective did any of the gathering try to settle down to talk with him.

But new arrivals were still drifting over. First

to arrive was Nigel's own ladyfriend, the dimpled Pamela.

"Ah Dumples!" Max grinned.

Moments later, Mavis arrived. "I'm very thankful you're here, Monsieur Dantan," she said, in a husky voice. "That poor boy, Tomas, will be persecuted if we don't do something to help him. And he's a perfect angel."

Pamela assented to that.

Miri felt that she ought to tell Dantan about the time Tomas came to her house and was not a perfect angel. If he had tried something similar with Maria there could have had very different consequences. But she was ashamed to tell him what had happened, and she certainly didn't want Seymour to hear about it. She could only hope he would solve the crime quickly and absolve Tomas. But if it began to look like the killer was Tomas, she would have to tell him after all. The thought made her very uncomfortable.

"A friend of mine," Mavis went on, "Vicente, who is a local, and knows everybody, has arranged for you to discreetly see the body. The police have stored it in the butcher's ice-house until releasing it to the family for burial. Vicente will escort you there."

"That would be interesting," Dantan said and

thanked her. "When will that be possible?"

"Later today. The fishermen go out before dawn, then in the early afternoon bring their catch to the *fondas* and restaurants, and if anything is left, they take it around to sell house by house. But lately there has been nothing left. The Hotel Palma Linda has been taking more and more of everyone's catch. It has become more popular as a restaurant for prosperous visitors, even those staying elsewhere. If you meet us here by five that will be early enough, but if Vicente is really busy it might be later. I'm sorry we can't say more precisely."

"That's perfectly all right. There are many people to meet and speak with, and this seems to be the place for that."

Lotte and Leo, a saturnine pair, had sat down slightly apart at the second table Liberto had drawn up as close as possible to the first. They gave Dantan intense nods. Dantan had not learned where this pair lived, or whether they had any opportunity to cross paths with the dead girl. He found himself wishing that they couldn't possibly have anything to do with the girl's death, as they looked impenetrable.

The Belge, Hugo, with a nod to Dantan, sat down beside the Germans at the second table. Liberto scurried out of the back room with hot chocolate and sweet rolls for him.

The well-upholstered Englishwomen, Dorcas and Hazel, then arrived, walking stiffly in their tight corsets. They were greeted warmly by their fellow Britons, Nigel and Pamela.

Lady Mary then descended on them with some dignity, and only a slight stagger. Nigel leaped up to hold her chair for her.

"What brings you out so early, Lady Mary?" Nigel asked jovially.

"The French detective," she said, enunciating with great deliberation, and with a gracious smile at Dantan. "I know nothing and I would adore hearing everything."

Harriet now hurried over, and Liberto instantly placed a glass of *manzanilla* before her. She barely touched it; it was information she sought and retailed at Liberto's; the *manzanilla* was her ostensible reason for being there. She began grilling Dantan, first about his previous cases, and then when that got nowhere, about his wife. Were there any children in the offing? Her interrogation technique was worthy of a professional! Since she was a grayhaired lady of a certain age he indulged her briefly, then turned the tables and began asking the questions.

"What do you know of the dead girl?"

"Nothing at all. Never go near that *fonda,* the

place always reeks of olive oil and garlic. But it's hard to fathom who would want to hurt an innocent child."

Harriet herself, despite her age, was an innocent if she knew nothing of what was too often done to innocent children.

"Without attributing motives to anyone, is there anyone you know of who might have come into contact with her from time to time?"

"No more than I'm sure you heard already. She worked at the *fonda* as a maid, did laundry on the side for some of the guests, cleaned house for Max and for Lady Mary – "

Here Lady Mary acknowledged this fact with a nod. "Poor thing," she sighed.

"Lady Mary, may I ask when was the last time Maria cleaned your house?"

Lady Mary furrowed her brow intensely. "Yesterday? The day before? No, surely that cannot be, she was dead already, poor child." She concentrated some more, but then shook her head sadly. "I'm so sorry. I really can't think."

"Shocking!" said Dorcas and Hazel in unison. But whether at Lady Mary's inability to think, or at the girl's death, was unclear.

"Had either of you ladies seen her lately?" Dantan asked them.

"Never seen 'er in me life," declared Dorcas.

Hazel nodded in agreement.

Two small thin men, introduced to Dantan as Edgar and Percy, were greeted by Nigel with the comment that it was good to see them, they hadn't been seen in these parts lately. Edgar and Percy both gave him simpering sour smiles.

Nigel made the pleasant announcement that the currency woes of the British colony had been solved. A relative of the arrested money-changer had taken over the business and they would be receiving their funds as usual. Of course, now that the British authorities knew more about the operation they might very well keep a closer watch, but the money-changer's customers had been assured by their new contact − indirectly, of course − that contingency plans were in place.

Eventually they drifted off one by one or two by two for the midday meal, assuring one another they would see one another later in the afternoon.

As this was a mail-delivery day it was likely that almost everyone would show up.

Cindy invited Judy to come to their house to see her husband's work. Judy looked at Miri. "Can you come with me?"

"Let's make it another time." Miri wanted to warn Judy first about Cindy's hard-sell tactics, and about Fred's work. She knew that the artist and his wife held exaggerated views of what it was worth. And of course Judy was the epitome of the gullible buyer. Miri would have to go along to protect her friend.

The Dantans' taxi was waiting, the driver having been hired by Judy to be her personal chauffeur while the Dantans were on Ibiza. Judy took off for the bumpy ride to the hotel, her invitation to ride along having been turned down by Miri, who set off for her house on her bicycle.

After five, Dantan returned to Liberto's for his rendezvous with Vicente. Judy considered remaining in their cool room, relaxing, but in the end was tempted by the gossip.

Miri pulled up her bicycle at Liberto's soon after. The same crowd, augmented by Claude, Hugo, Francine, Jorgen, and the bearded American writer Max. Everyone, however antisocial, seemed to yearn for mail.

Miri was one of the first to get on line at the post-office door, not that she was expecting anything special, but she never knew when a letter from Charlie Nugent might arrive, once again telling her that her old job would be open for her if she should decide to come back. Not that she wanted to, but it was a good feeling that they wanted her. Maybe by the time her money ran out she might consider going back to work in Paris again for awhile.

Miri had given up hoping that Vanessa Tate, a friend from her early Paris days, now back in the States, would write. She had written once, and Miri had answered, and hadn't heard from her since.

Miri's monthly money order for the forty dollars from her post-office account was not due yet, but she could always hope. A few more dinners at Hotel Palma Linda and she might have to increase it to forty-five.

It was therefore a somewhat alarming surprise when the young postal clerk handed her a telegram. She ripped open the buff envelope, expecting bad news. But this was not bad news. It was from Seymour. That morning he had received her letter. "Got a short leave. All set to come to Ibiza immediately. Am flying to Barcelona today! Will be taking overnight boat from to Ibiza to arrive tomorrow, Saturday morning. Love, Seymour."

Back at the cafe, everyone who wasn't reading his mail was talking about the murder. While Liberto continually appeared with trays of drinks, Miri found an opportunity to hand Seymour's telegram to Judy without being observed.

Judy squealed with delight. "This is terrific! Maybe he'll propose again!"

"What makes you think that would be so terrific?" Miri asked truculently. But secretly she started thinking maybe that wouldn't be so bad, after all.

Pamela told Dantan perkily, "We've found out some useful things for you. Mavis here, for instance, is sleeping with an Ibizan fisherman" – here Mavis blushed and a few of the others chuckled – "and he has arranged for you to see the body!"

Dantan looked politely interested although he had already heard this from Nigel and Mavis herself, and was in fact awaiting the arrival of Vicente to escort him to the ice-house where the body was being stored.

"Her boyfriend Vicente," Pamela went on obliviously, "Vicente found out that the police had stored Maria's body in the butcher's ice-house until the mainland *Guardia Civil* could come and take it away, or release it to Maria's family for burial. The local police are so busy looking for Tomas they haven't paid any attention to the victim! The body is just lying there along with the scrawny lamb carcasses and goats' testicles."

Dantan nodded acknowledgement.

"And Harriet here --"

Harriet now spoke up for herself. "I've already talked to Tomas Bonet's sister, Catalina – they both speak excellent English – and I've asked her to round up all the Ibizan maids who knew Maria and she got them to agree to be questioned. Most of them don't speak Spanish, only Ibicencan, but Catalina will translate for everyone. It will have to be somewhere where it looks natural, so that those hideous policemen won't notice anything suspicious. I'll chaperone. For of course the single girls can't meet with a man without a chaperone."

Dantan did not think this was an ideal arrangement, having the sister of the suspect be so involved in the investigation, but the damage had been done.

Pamela said, "We've tentatively arranged it for Sunday evening, during the *paseo* or maybe when the movie breaks up and everyone is talking at once anyway. Consuelo, Maria's sister, works at the *Fonda Bahia* where Maria worked, and will get all the other maids there, too."

Mavis said quietly, "Vicente has lined up a number of Ibizan men for you to question if you wish. The coal-stoker at the *fonda*, the fishermen who were at the wharf the night the body might have been carried to Tomas' truck...."

Dantan smiled to himself. This crowd of busybodies was doing quite well without him.

"Does anybody have any theories about who might have committed this alleged murder?" Dantan looked from face to face. They all shook their heads.

Pamela spoke up. "None of us think it could be Tomas Bonet."

"I don't know about that," Max growled. "If he didn't do it, then why was her body found beside his truck?"

Murmurs of protest went around the crowd.

"Simply that someone else could have put it there," said Dantan, aware that if that were so the motive for doing so was not yet known.

Claude had said nothing to this point, but now voiced a few words to Dantan in French just to establish a friendly contact, and rescue him from the continual grilling by the others. Moving his chair behind Dantan (there was no room to squeeze in beside him), Claude began to talk quietly to the Inspector. He was eager to tell a fellow Frenchman of his idea of starting a quality French restaurant right here in San Marino, and asked Dantan to give his opinion, once he had gotten a feel of the place. He mentioned the spot in mind, down near the fishermen's wharf. There was a local restaurant there now, called Pedro's, but it was sparsely patronized.

Mavis, who also spoke French had followed this exchange. She said, "It's so dreary down there."

Claude said, "Oh I'll change all that, with outdoor torches and colored lights and a Victrola playing lilting French songs, Pierre Brasseur, Edith Piaf, like that. And of course the food will be *formidable.*"

"How does the food there now compare to the food at the Hotel Palma Linda? That's where my wife and I are staying."

"The hotel food is much better, right now –"

"Then why go somewhere else?" Miri interrupted bluntly.

"It's worth trying for the atmosphere and sampling local dishes."

Dantan hastily remarked, "We should try local things."

"We should?" Judy said. "I like the Hotel Palma Linda's food. We got a great English breakfast this morning. And lunch is good too. And I'll bet the kitchen at the hotel is cleaner."

"If I were to advise you, Claude, which I am not presuming to do," said Mavis, "I would suggest that rather than take over a dingy dockside place, install your quality French restaurant right in the Hotel Palma Linda, where the guests are the most prosperous tourists who come to San Marino. If it's truly good then it should bring additional business to the hotel."

Mavis explained to Dantan, in charmingly Australian-accented French, that she and Claude had dined at Pedro's the previous Sunday night and except for a raucous party going on among the fishermen, the dock was deserted. Dark and deserted.

Claude said impatiently, "As I have said, I would brighten things up."

Mavis did not look happy.

Dantan asked, in English so that others at the table could be included, "Wasn't early Monday morning when Tomas Bonet found the girl's body beside his truck? And wasn't his truck parked near the fishermen's wharf?"

"Not far," said Nigel.

Mavis said angrily, "I refuse to believe that any of the fishermen had anything to do with the murder. They are all decent men."

Pamela said with a vicious smile, "How do you know? Have you slept with all of them?"

This was so rude that no one smiled except Cindy, who exchanged smirks with Pamela.

A rise in the emotional tone was averted as Pamela let out a loud squeal of delight. She had turned to the English papers she had received, several days out of date, and had come upon the article about their money-changer having landed in jail. Thanks to Lady Mary's superior sources of intelligence, the Brits knew that that problem had been dealt with, but the tardy newspapers did not yet reflect that happy news.

Lotte and Leo departed with their mail, as did Fred and Cindy.

Jorgen had positioned himself beside Miri, the Belge beside Harriet, and Claude and Francine joined Dantan.

Edgar and Percy flipped quickly through their letters, scanning return addresses, then tucked them all into a straw shopping basket. Percy twittered over one envelope, which he insisted on opening over Edgar's protests, because it was from "a special friend" of Marilyn, Beezlebub and Marlene (their cats, Harriet explained). He displayed it to the group at large, of whom only Harriet took more than a token look. It was a birthday card embellished with a grinning winking cartoon cat and addressed to Marlene. They then rose to leave with a "Cheerio" to Dorcas and Hazel.

Harriet did her best to observe the source of the others' letters, but was limited by their modest efforts at maintaining privacy, and her own short-sightedness.

Dantan wanted to ask questions of the *fonda* guests, but there was no opportunity to do so discreetly. Francine, staying at the *fonda*, was available, but he was dubious of her ability to be forthcoming with anything useful. And in his mind she certainly was not a suspect! The worst thing he had heard about this delicate creature was that she had an on-off relationship with a burly bad-tempered writer, Max, who sometimes knocked her around.

Jorgen was trying to engage Miri in conversation. Dantan thought it would be a favor to her if he interrupted, and he might be able to ask the "Great Dane" a few questions. He asked, first of all, how Jorgen liked the *fonda*.

Jorgen frowned. "It is convenient."

"You take your meals there?"

"Yes. It is convenient."

"How's the food?" Dantan asked conversationally.

"Digestible." Jorgen let out a booming laugh. "If I want to eat well I go back to my homeland. Unfortunately I cannot afford to pay to eat in Sweden. An orange would be five *krona*, forty *pesetas*. *La condition humaine, n'est-pas?*" Again he boomed a laugh. Apparently he was his own best source of entertainment. He lifted his cognac glass to Dantan. "*Skol.*" He tossed it off in one swallow.

"About that the young girl who was murdered... "

"Very sad."

"Any idea how it happened?"

Jorgen made a wringing motion with his

hands as if strangling someone.

Dantan was startled.

Jorgen laughed. "I have performed that many times on chickens. My parents have a small farm and I was the official strangler. In fact, I have aided the cook here several times when they were short-handed in the kitchen." He said more soberly, "I have heard that she was strangled."

Jorgen then rose, gave Dantan a slight bow, picked up his letters and newspapers and begin to stride off.

"Wait!" Dantan called to him.

Jorgen looked at him questioningly.

"I wonder if you could help me out for a few minutes? You may know that some of the English have asked me to try to find out what I can about the maid's death, and I am trying to gather whatever information I can about her habits, and behavior, and the like. Since she worked in the *fonda*...."

Jorgen said, "I want to get back to my work. However, you are welcome to come with me to my studio and pose your questions until I kick you out!"

"Thank you!" Dantan promptly followed after him.

EIGHT

A BASEMENT STUDIO

Jorgen began rewetting cloths to place on some clay pieces in progress. Dantan was grateful that the sculptor was not yet in a creative frenzy. He even seemed pleased to show Dantan his work. He had commissions from a group of dentists in Stockholm, who sent him a monthly allowance for which he would eventually have to deliver a piece of art to each.

He agreed to answer some questions. "But I want to assure you, *Monsieur l'Inspecteur*," he grinned, "I had no hand in the death of the maiden."

Dantan looked around Jorgen's studio, a large space in the basement of the *fonda,* and was somewhat surprised at its dimness. The light came only from four narrow windows above eye-level. It was almost like a prison-cell.

Jorgen's studio occupied three-quarters of the basement. The rest of the space was taken up by two other functions of the *fonda*: the coal-fire which heated all the hot water for the place, together with a coal-heap in one corner.

Part of the basement was also used as a laundry. Here were a small coal-stove and a rudimentary laundry: huge tubs, scrubbing-boards, hand-wringers nailed over one of the tubs. Large empty baskets were in a pile, presumably to bring and deliver the laundry. Four irons sat on a table near the coal-stove, suggesting that they were heated on that coal-stove before use. A strange setting indeed for an artist's studio.

Dantan asked Jorgen when was the last time he recalled seeing Maria.

"Sunday afternoon. She was doing laundry. I was hard at work and barely noticed her."

"Were you still at work when she left? Or was she still at work when you left?"

"I did not notice."

"You two didn't speak at all?"

"Not at all. We were each intent on getting our respective work done."

"Did you two ever converse?"

"No."

"On Sunday, did she hang up the laundry she had been doing while you were there?"

"I don't know. I didn't notice when she left. But I don't remember seeing any laundry flapping on the line the next morning."

"You would have noticed that?"

"Assuredly. When there is laundry on the lines I have to push my way through it leaving the basement, the lines are very near my door. And I have to go out the door before I can go up the outside stairs to the dining-room.

"There might have been a basketful of clothes on the floor when I left to go upstairs to my room, but I'm not sure."

""Was it usual that she did laundry Sunday afternoons?"

"The girls took extra work from guests sometimes. The *fonda's* laundry was done during the week."

"Do you know whose laundry she was doing?"

"No."

"What did you do after you finished work for the day, on Sunday?"

"Ate at the *fonda,* then roamed the village,

stared at the girls, drank."

"Was Maria one of the girls you stared at?"

"I only look at the ones with bosoms. And that's hard enough to see, I can tell you!" Jorgen guffawed. "The way they push the two tits together and wrap them in cloths as if there is only one! Odd custom. And now if you'll excuse me...."

Dantan left the basement, his eyes dazzled by the sudden sunlight. Jorgen has a point, working in semi-darkness, Dantan thought.

When Dantan returned to the cafe Miri said to him, "That Jorgen is an interesting sculptor, but he's weird."

"In what way?"

"He likes to joke about strangling chickens."

Judy said, "His looks are really something! I wouldn't want to meet that hulk in a dark alley."

"I believe he's a lamb," said Harriet.

Dantan now pulled his chair closer to the Belgian.

"How do you like the *fonda*?" Dantan asked him in French.

Hugo shrugged. "I'm thinking of renting a house." He responded in French, but with a Flemish accent.

"Are you bored in San Marino?"

"Not in San Marino in particular. I'm bored

everywhere." The Belge then turned red, perhaps ashamed of so much self-revelation.

"Do you get to the Sunday movie much?"

"Sometimes."

"Did you happen to go last week?"

Hugo stared blankly through his pig-eyes at Dantan, then said, "Yes."

"How was the show?"

"Stupid, as usual."

"What was it?"

The Belgian wrinkled his nose in thought for a moment. "Those movies are not very memorable, you know. I do remember something, though. A mail-order bride comes out to a jungle plantation invaded by swarms of destructive ants. Not my cup of tea."

Dantan found that exceedingly interesting.

"Wasn't it terrible about the death of that maid at the *fonda*?"

"Yes."

"Did you know her?"

"Of course I did," Hugo said angrily. "She cleaned my room every day."

"Did she clean it Sunday?"

"I suppose so."

"Did you see her Sunday?"

"I don't remember," he said impatiently.

"Had I known she was going to get herself killed I would have made a note. And what business is it of yours in any case?"

"Simple human curiosity. I apologize if I have offended you."

"See here, I don't care much for being quizzed as if you were suspicious of me." He rose clumsily, rocking and almost knocking over the table as he did so.

"Well, did you? See the girl Sunday?" Nigel persisted in a pleasant but firm tone.

But Hugo was stalking off.

"An odd man," Nigel murmured to Dantan. "Not very prepossessing."

Dantan refrained from remarking that that statement could have been made about many of the foreign residents here. But that didn't make them murderers. He would have to take a closer look at the locals. The fishermen partying that Sunday night might have lured Maria there. And always, he returned to the thought of Tomas himself....

He asked Claude to accompany him to Pedro's, to assist in questioning the restaurant employees.

Pedro was extremely cordial, and agreeable to Claude's request to summon each of his employees for questioning. Like all the other locals he had been appalled by the murder, and convinced that Tomas Bonet had nothing to do with it. He was eager to do whatever he could to help solve the crime, as long as it did not land him in the suspicious sights of the *Guardia Civil.*

Despite Pedro's great willingness to help, matters moved painfully slowly and, in Dantan's opinion, inefficiently. After a series of laborious translations from Dantan's French to Claude and Claude's Spanish to Pedro and Pedro's Ibicencan to each of his employees, the results were basically useless. The cook had seen or heard nothing out of the ordinary, the coal-stoker the same, the waiter nothing. Pedro himself had lavished his attentions on Claude's party and a discussion of possible mutual business.

"Are they the only ones who work here?" Dantan asked testily.

Claude repeated the question.

Pedro said, "And the garbage-man. He's not here at this moment. But he won't know anything."

When Dantan and Nigel arrived back at Liberto's cafe, the large table was crowded with expatriates, but only the men. Claude explained that all the women had gone off shopping at the convent. Dantan had known that Judy and Miri were planning to go but hadn't known what a unique and important event was taking place there.

One of the Englishwomen had managed to persuade the nuns that their needlework was so exquisite that they could raise money for the Church by making and selling, not just little items that had been specially ordered, but quantities to put up for sale. This persuasion took some doing. The nuns abhorred the thought of being involved in commerce. They saw the work they did as special favors for individuals. In the end, it was Catalina who persuaded the nuns.

She promised them to provide at cost, all embroidery silks and the delicate linens and batistes they needed and would take back anything they didn't use so they wouldn't be charged for it.

The Englishwomen promised that they would help sell whatever the nuns produced.

The American women promised to buy everything.

Most of the men were taking the opportunity of the women's absence to make genial fun of the females for their shopping cravings. Max, however, was angry for an obscure reason. "There's entirely too much fraternization taking place between the locals and us foreigners. We're corrupting them. They live an utterly simple, almost Biblical way, with which they are resigned, if not satisfied, and we're making them discontented, but not enough to do anything about it."

"I haven't noticed a greal deal of fraternization," Claude said coolly.

"Ha! You're one of the worst, with your restaurant with colored lights and French waltzes.... Soon you'll be cohabiting with one of your waitresses!"

This was patently unreasonable. Claude was not planning to have any waitresses, and in fact intended to have only male waiters.

"You don't approve of Mavis' love affair, I suppose, with Vicente."

"Damn right, I don't. Someone's going to get hurt.'"

Dantan, as did the others, forebore from saying that in Max' own relationship with a woman, though not a local, someone was always getting hurt – and by him.

"Then you think Maria's death was caused by one of us?"

"I still think Tomas did it," Max grumbled.

Nigel turned to Jorgen. "What do you think of that, old boy?"

Jorgen let out a belly laugh and tossed off his cognac.

NINE

THE ICE-HOUSE

Dantan made sure he had Judy's nail-scissors and tweezers, the packet of glassine envelopes he had packed in Paris, two colored wax pencils, and a number of cotton-tipped swaps in their own envelope. Several pairs of white cotton gloves completed his forensic-evidence kit.

After returning from the wharf with Claude, he had a considerable wait for the Ibizan fisherman, Vicente, to arrive. Vicente had a weatherbeaten face and carved features. He shot an intense look at Mavis, who returned it with a fond gaze. Vicente spoke only Ibicencan, Mavis not much Spanish, but the two managed to communicate with looks and signs.

"Vicente will take you now to the butcher's ice-house to see the body," Mavis said.

Dantan nodded his thanks, then accompanied Vicente in silence through a narrow uphill street of small white houses with storefronts below. Vicente and Dantan entered the butcher's small shop. On wall hooks were three sets of goats' testicles and a lamb carcass. The butcher was alone, in a bloody white apron. He led them wordlessly through a rear door to a small room considerably cooler than the first, cool enough to make the men shiver. A heavy wooden table engrained with dried blood occupied most of the little room. A meat cleaver and other metal implements were on the table. In one corner was a large ice-box. On the floor next to it was a form wrapped in a white sheet.

The butcher removed the cleaver and other tools from the table, then lifted the body from the floor onto his carving-table, and pulled back the sheet, as professionally as if he were an attendant in a morgue. The body was pathetically thin. Maria's dark hair half covered her face. Dantan could see bruises around her neck that were consistent with her having been strangled.

She was wearing a black pinafore. It appeared to Dantan that the pinafore was on inside out as its seams were exposed. Small bits of white fuzz dotted the fabric. Dantan removed a pair of clean white cotton gloves from his kit, pulled them on, and with the tweezers picked up some of the fuzz and placed it into a glassine envelope, on which he wrote a code with a red wax pencil.

The butcher excused himself to tend his shop, leaving Vicente and Dantan in the ice-room.

Dantan gently lifted the black pinafore. The girl was not wearing underpants, and there were bruises around the vaginal area. With a cotton swab, Dantan gingerly swapped the outside of the vagina, where bruising had appeared. These swabs, too, went into a glassine envelope. Vicente looked away while Dantan was conducting this examination. Dantan then examined as much as he could of the right side of the pinafore without actually removing it. There he discovered an encrusted brown spot, a portion of which he scraped into another glassine envelope, coding it.

Dantan would send these samples to Jean-Jacques in Paris. Jean-Jacques would do some basic analysis himself, at home, on his own time, with simple forensic tools which he kept in order to familiarize himself more and more with the processes. If there was anything that seemed to him to merit more in-depth analysis, he would ask Chief Inspector Goulette for permission to have it done at the

Police Judiciare, but that would take longer and he wouldn't be able to reply to Dantan as quickly.

But before sending these samples to Jean-Jacques, Dantan would first see what other physical evidence he could collect.

He gently replaced the sheet over the body. He and Vicente left in silence. Vicente touched his straw hat to Dantan at the door and departed.

Dantan wondered what the doctor had discovered. And whether he would be willing to impart any of it to a stranger. Dantan could not present himself to the doctor as any kind of investigator; that information would be relayed immediately to the police. Whatever he might learn, he had to obtain in some casual guise.

Dantan could see how useful it would be to get some samples taken from various rooms in the *fonda*. Besides his friendly contact with Claude, who lived there, he might, with the help of Catalina, get Consuelo to do some evidence-collecting around the place.

Back at the cafe, Dantan sat down beside Nigel. "You've seen the body?" Nigel asked.

"Yes. Pathetic. I need your help. I would like one of the maids, if possible, to collect some physical samples from rooms at the *fonda*."

"Quite simple. This is a job for the women.

With Catalina's help, Pamela and Mavis have already spoken to one of the maids at the *fonda,* Consuelo, the dead girl's sister, is eager to help. Sunday night when everyone is milling around, Catalina will be there. You can question the maids and give Consuelo instructions."

"Now that I've seen the girl's body, it would also be extremely useful if I could speak with the doctor."

"Don't expect him to be helpful," responded Nigel. "In fact it might be risky for you if he surmised that you are looking into this matter. For one thing, the doctor is reputed to be very incompetent, and he may himself have done something to Maria, clumsily, to be sure, not deliberately, which caused her death. She might not have been dead when she was brought there. He certainly wouldn't want that to come out. Secondly he is close with the police – remember he is the one who put them onto Tomas – so an investigation to find some other perpetrator would implicitly cast doubt on his judgment.... The best approach I can think to recommend is a social one. You and your wife are obviously prosperous travellers, and if some way could be found to convey that you want to meet with professionals such as himself...."

Dantan was dubious, not that the social angle

wouldn't work, but that they could not accomplish such a contact. "Perhaps my wife will be able to think of how to do this."

Nigel laughed. "You could always invent some illness and consult him about it, but given his reputation he might administer something lethal!"

"It would also be helpful," Dantan said, "to question with each of the workers at the *fonda*, as well as the guests boarding there."

"Quite right," said Nigel. "Jorgen, Hugo, Francine, Claude, are all boarding there. That will be easy. They're often around. In the meantime, until you can get those other things done, feel free to sit down and grill any of us. Cindy acts as Fred's watch-dog, so expect her to be there at all times. And when you talk to Fred be sure your wife is no-where to be seen," Nigel laughed, "or Cindy will make short shrift of your visit."

Dantan said, "Miri is going to be taking my wife to look at Fred's paintings. Judy is becoming a collector in a small way, and Miri had been helping her in finding and judging work."

"Well that may ingratiate her a bit with Cindy — she is her husband's biggest booster — but your wife is a dish, and Cindy will worry about that."

Dantan said, "With Miri present Fred can't get very far."

Nigel grinned. "Miri is a dish too, but you have to use your imagination to spot it under those oversized men's undershirts and baggy dungarees she always wears."

The next morning Miri and Judy went to visit Fred's studio. As predicted, Fred was chaperoned by his wife Cindy.

Judy gazed at each huge painting slowly, silently, and expressionlessly. She was waiting to show enthusiasm if Miri did. But she liked them. She found the hodge-podge of brilliant colors engaging, and could imagine one brightening up their dark dining-room with the lugubrious antique furniture. Until they had a baby. Then she would hang it in the nursery. Babies were supposed to like bright colors.

Miri was gazing at the paintings too, but Cindy was concentrated on Judy. She was the one with fat wallet. "Well? Aren't they brilliant? The most original thing you've ever seen?"

"Jackson Pollock paints that way too," Miri pointed out.

Cindy sniffed. "He uses a similar technique, but the paintings are not comparable."

"What are the prices?" Miri asked coolly.

Cindy clearly would have preferred that the question come from Judy, to whom she probably would have quoted higher, but she said, "One thousand dollars each."

Miri thought that was way too much. She could live in San Marino for over a year on a thousand dollars.

But Judy said, "I'll think about it."

When they left, Judy said, "I liked them."

"I could see that."

"You could? I wasn't showing any interest."

"That's why. You're usually so bubbly over everything that when you weren't I knew you were hiding your feelings."

Judy giggling, they climbed into their taxi to be driven half-way around the bay to the Hotel Palma Linda. Dantan, who was still talking with the expatriates at the cafe, would have to make due with walking.

Judy insisted once more that Miri lunch with them at the hotel. She would tolerate the sun and the heat in the morning, at the cafe or going shopping, but insisted on shutting herself up in her air-conditioned suite for the rest of the afternoon.

Ater the women had left, Claude strolled over the table and greeted Dantan, asking him how it was going. It occurred to Dantan that Claude might help him investigate at the *fonda* too.

"Come back there now," Claude said. "It will soon be mealtime and guests will be going to the dining-room. We'll have a look around the whole place."

First they climbed the outside staircase to Claude's small immaculate room on the second floor. It had a tiny balcony overlooking the street. On the bed was a natural-colored woolen blanket. It was made of uncured wool, that is, with the natural lanolin still in , and it itched like the devil and was much too warm for this climate. With Judy's nail-scissors Dantan cut a snippet from the blanket, put it in a glassine envelope and wrote a code number on it as he had done with each of his other samples.

The rooms of Hugo, Francine, and Jorgen were on the third floor, so Dantan decided to leave the snippet collection to Consuelo, to avoid encountering anyone.

Claude invited Dantan to join him for the midday meal at the *fonda*, but Dantan had promised his wife that he would lunch with her and Miri at their hotel. He invited Claude to join them, but was graciously turned down.

Over a delicious seafood salad of locally-caught shrimp and lobster and chunks of a white meaty fish which Miri refrained from telling Judy was eel, Dantan told them briefly, and without details, of having seen the victim's body. "It would be very useful to talk with the doctor." He related what Nigel had said that had discouraged him from thinking he could. "Nigel thinks my best bet is to meet the doctor socially, somehow. The problem is that none of the foreigners socialize with him, and some of them, like Cindy and Fred, actively hate him."

They all pondered this for a moment.

Then Miri said dubiously, "Maybe Dorcas and Hazel play bridge with him and one of his friends. They love bridge. I know they have a Thursday game with Percy and Edgar. Maybe they have a regular game with the doctor too. I could drop in on them later today, when it's cooled down enough for Hazel to be tending her roses, and ask her. Can you believe she grows roses? It's so hot and dry, but they're her babies, and she has made sunshades for them out of beach umbrellas, and waters them by hand. She has three rosebushes, one deep red, one pale pink, and one white. " Miri suddenly brightened. "Maybe I'll ask her if I can do a painting of her working on her roses!" It was sad, an aging woman far from home trying to grow roses in an inhospitable place, arid and too hot. Miri wondered for a moment if by painting in such an environment she too was trying to "grow roses" in an inhospitable place?

"Ooh, that would be good," said Judy. "Some

of the others you've done here are so sad."

"Well that was the idea. But I like this idea, too. I just don't like the thought of meeting up with their dog, an ugly Ibizan-hound with a big pink nose."

""Are you allergic to it?"

"No, I just don't like it sniffing at me."

"Too bad you're not allergic. Remember how you thought you had a bad cold at Madame Fleuris' when it turned out to be you were allergic to Gervaise's cat?* If you could only get a sneezing fit we'd have an excuse to take you to the doctor."

"But Edgar and Percy have cats! Whenever they've been around they talked about those infernal cats."

"Then that's it!" Judy said. "You have to visit them and pet their cats until you start sneezing, then Alphie and I will take you to consult the doctor and say you have a bad case of the flu."

Dantan liked this idea.

"The trouble is, they're nasty, those two, the Twit and the Twerp as Max calls them, but I'll do it in the interests of justice. I'll go this afternoon, before I change my mind."

"No," Dantan said, "first we need to find out

*see A MURDER OF CONVENIENCE

what the doctor's office hours are, so you can get the exposure to the cats just before. We may have to wait until Monday to try to see him."

"I'll drop in on Dorcas and Hazel later today, when the sun is lower, and find out if they socialize with the doctor."

In the late afternoon, Miri rode her Velo-Solex down past the Hotel Palma Linda. Off the dirt road, not yet in the village, was the Englishwomen's house.

Dorcas was out front, pumping water into a bucket. She was wearing a shapeless blue cotton dress, and was sweating profusely. "Well hello there, Miri. I'm just slaking the insatiable thirst of Hazel's thorny friends! Must see to them before we do to ourselves! Go out back where Hazel is fussing with her roses and tell her I've gotten her a bucketful of water. "

Miri went out back where plump Hazel, in a big straw hat and thick gardening gloves, was doing something to what seemed to Miri to be perfect plants, with perfect blossoms. "I just came by to see the roses," she said.

"Aren't they delightful? Go inside and I'll be in in a moment to make some tea."

Miri didn't need to relay Dorcas' message as that lady herself came along lugging a bucket of water and set it down near the roses.

"Lovely! Thanks dear!

"Now Hazel love, shall we have some tea?"

"When they were settled around a low table on which Hazel had placed teaput, sugar, milk from powdered milk, cups, and English biscuits from a tin, Miri said abruptly, "Hazel, I would like to do a painting of you with your roses." Mabel, the pink-nosed hound, was sniffing at her feet. She tried to ignore it.

"What a lovely idea!" enthused Dorcas.

Hazel willingly agreed. "When would you like to do it?"

"As soon as my friends have left San Marino. They're only here for a short stay. I may want to do a few sketches earlier."

"Any time, love."

"Except Thursdays," Miri laughed. "I know you play bridge on Thursdays."

"Quite right."

"Do you have any other regular bridge games?"

"None. Once per week is quite enough."

"Do you socialize with any of the Ibizans?" Miri asked. "The educated ones, I mean, like the doctor?"

"Gracious no, love, there are quite enough

English here."

Miri thanked them for the tea and promised to let them know when her friends had left the island, so that she could start the painting.

TEN

DEBARKATIONS

Seymour Levin was to arrive from Paris on Saturday morning, just two days after the Dantans had gotten to the island. As soon as he had received Miri's letter on Thursday he moved swiftly to investigate airplanes and boats. He found a flight from Paris to Barcelona for the very next day, Friday. He could then take the overnight boat from Barcelona to Ibiza. He had no difficulty in getting a seat on the airplane, but all berths on the boat had been booked long in advance so he had to settle for a seat on the deck all night.

He sent a telegram to Miri care of the post-office where she picked up her mail to expect him to arrive on Saturday morning, packed a small bag, then went to the PX where he bought a pretty piece of antique Bohemian garnet jewelry for her. Nothing that would frighten her as the ring had done, just a little bird of gold filigree filled in with garnets. If things went well, he would look for the ring he had misplaced when she had returned it, and try again. But for now, he was going to keep a slight air of detachment.

Early Saturday morning, he shook the sleepiness from his bones, picked up his small bag from beside his deck-chair, and went to the gangway. Here he was joined by a horde of other travellers of all sorts, from peasants wrapped in yards of coarse black cotton to foreigners, some smart-looking, some scruffy. A few *Guardia Civil* wandered around the deck, looking, in their ludicrously-overdone green uniforms and black patent leather tricornes, as if they would have burst into song, were it not for their glowering expressions. They peered in a bored way into travellers' bags. They did not seem to expect to find any guns or contraband in this crowd.

Miri, Judy and Dantan were at the wharf in Ibiza to greet Seymour. Judy was now wearing another of her new sleeveless linen sheaths made especially for her trip, this one in pink, with matching pink sandals.

They were in a crowd, mostly locals, who liked to turn out for the arrival of every boat, whether they knew anyone on board or not. The arrival of an overnight boat, two per week from Barcelona, one from Palma and one from Alicante, was a big event in a place where almost nothing ever happened.

Seymour's three friends were waving to him as he wended his way down the gangway, then suddenly Miri stopped waving and started talking animatedly to Dantan, pointing to someone else debarking. Dantan broke away from the two young women, prepared to catch up to the other individual as soon as he set foot on the ground.

Seymour gave Miri a big hug right on the wharf, much to her embarassment, although it made her feel good, and he greeted Judy with a big grin. "Where's Dantan? I saw him with you a moment ago."

"He'll be with us in a minute. He spotted someone he knew and wanted to catch him before he got away."

Dantan did join them very soon. He and Seymour shook hands. "Let's go get some coffee," Dantan proposed.

"And food," Judy added.

This suited Seymour, who was ravenous. He

had eaten quickly and lightly the night before. Not having the patience to wait for the restaurants to open at nine or later, when the Spaniards began their late dinners, he had settled for *tapas* and beer. The next morning, the coffee and buns available on the boat had not been enough to fill the void in his stomach. He wanted real food. Miri knew of a cafe near the wharf accustomed to the eccentric tastes of foreigners, who might want eggs for breakfast. The cafe could always turn out eggs fried in olive oil, with thick fatty bacon, and strong coffee with condensed milk in a tube from Switzerland always kept on hand for the *extranjeros*. The waiter placed a basket of oranges on the table and everyone reached for one. The fragrance when the skin was pierced was intoxicating.

"Did you get to have a word with him?" Miri asked Dantan in a low voice. For it was Tomas Bonet Miri had spotted descending from the Barcelona boat, and had hastily whispered that information to Dantan. She herself wanted to avoid Tomas if possible, and was depending upon Dantan to introduce himself and carry on without her.

Dantan nodded. "I explained briefly who I was. He seemed to know all about my coming down from Paris and was not at all surprised. Although he's been hanging out, if not hiding out, in

Barcelona, he seemed well informed of events relating to his own situation.

"We agreed to meet this evening, right in San Marino. I'll tell you more when we get back to our hotel." He turned to Seymour. "How long are you here for, *mon vieux*?" Dantan asked him.

Seymour smiled at Miri. "Depends on her. I got a week's leave."

Judy beamed at them both.

"Any ideas where I could stay?" Seymour looked at Miri hopefully.

"I recommend the *Fonda Bahia* in San Marino," Miri said stiffly. "The owners are probably Nazis, but the food is good." She had no intention of inviting him to stay at her house, although she hoped he would come over and visit from time to time.

Afer Seymour had downed a heavy greasy breakfast accompanied by thick coffee strong enough to dissolve paint, and the others picked at the fragrant oranges, they jumped into the ancient taxi whose driver had been waiting patiently to return them to San Marino. Dantan had cautioned the girls to say nothing of the murder while in the taxi but to wait until the four of them were alone. He didn't want gossip relayed among the locals who might repeat, possibly erroneously, anything he said.

Dantan sat himself beside the driver. In the back, Judy and Seymour flanked Miri. Seymour took Miri's hand and it was not pulled away.

They rattled off. Judy asked Seymour what he had seen in Barcelona, and whether he thought it was worth her taking a trip there for shopping.

Miri laughed, "It's always worth it for you to go shopping anywhere, you could find things you wanted even in the desert!"

Judy giggled and did not deny it.

Seymour was of no assistance. The only thing he had gone to see after leaving the airplane was the *Sagrada Familia*, the unfinished cathedral designed by Gaudi. In fact, he now pulled from his bag a small soft-covered book on Gaudi, with many colored pictures, that he had picked up for Miri. It seemed like ESP, she had been thinking recently about Gaudi, too!

Seymour looked out at the passing scene, the arid fields of scrub interspersed with almond groves, without comment. Coming from the opposite direction was a black-suited peasant with big straw hat riding in a crude horse-drawn carriage. "It will probably take him most of the day to get to town," Miri remarked.

"'I'd love to buy a hat like that," Judy said.

"That's easy. They're everywhere, and very

cheap. And you can get a pair of *alpargatas* while you're at it — " Miri stuck forward a foot on which was a black canvas espadrille with woven straw soles. "They're good for walking on dirt roads and also very cheap."

Judy giggled. "I don't plan on doing much walking on dirt roads."

A little later a rickety bus with a few passengers came along, also from the direction of San Marino, and having passed the taxi, honked its horn loudly as it passed the horse and cart, and then rumbled along at a more modern speed.

Halfway to San Marino, they came upon the roadside shop where Inez, *Señor* Bonet's daughter, had first told Miri about the house she eventually rented. All agreed to stop and buy sodas and say hello. Inez told them that since the police had been looking for him, her cousin Tomas had gone to Barcelona "on business" for awhile.

In San Marino, the first thing the foursome did was to go to the *Fonda Bahia* to see if there was a room for Seymour. Ilse, one of the owners, with a heavy German accent, greeted them with uncharacteristic warmth. She certainly did have an excellent room for the American. He was most welcome. The four of them followed her up one flight of the outside narrow stone stairs to the second floor.

"Don't you have something up higher, *Señora?*" Miri asked. "In this room the cooking smells are strong."

Ilse looked annoyed but agreed that she did have a room on the next floor up. The room there was about equal in size to the first one, and did not smell as strongly of pungent olive oil and garlic. But it was not fragrance-free! Seymour, however, said it was okay, he would take it right away. Dropping his bag on the low table near the one armchair, he invited the others to be his guests at lunch at the *fonda*. Judy, however insisted that he and Miri come back with her and Dantan to their hotel for lunch. The food was excellent, their suite, where they could be served, was air-conditioned and, she added when Ilse had left the room to call a maid to put fresh sheets on the bed, they could talk privately.

A thin young girl with black hair tied back and wearing a black pinafore similar to the one Dantan had seen in the ice-house worn by Maria came along promptly, carrying a stack of clean sheets and towels. She greeted them diffidently.

"Very sad about Maria," Judy spoke up.

The maid didn't understand English, but at the word "Maria" tears welled up in her eyes. "*Mi hermana.*"

"Her sister," Miri said.

"Very sad," Judy sighed, her tone conveying her sympathy although the girl did not understand the words.

"Ask her when was the last time she saw her sister, and where," said Dantan.

But while Miri was trying to frame the question in her awkward Spanish, Ilse came back into the room. "Consuelo," she began and rattled off something commanding in German-accented Spanish, defeating Miri's ability to decipher it. Then Ilse handed Seymour a key, remarking, "Don't worry if you forget to lock the room, nobody takes anything."

"That's reassuring," Judy giggled, "they don't steal anything, they only kill people."

Ilse chose not to hear that. "*Senor* Levin, will you be taking the mid-day meal here?" she asked Seymour.

"Sometimes. I hope that's all right. But not today."

Ilse nodded, and as she seemed to waiting for them to leave before she did, they had no choice but to go out of the room without further conversation with Consuelo.

In the passageway onto which all the guest-rooms on that floor opened, they met two of the guests just on their way out. One was Hugo the Belgian, carrying a large stuffed gray sack. He smiled at them fatuously. "My laundry." The other was the redheaded redbearded giant Jorgen, carrying an identical sack, but empty. He nodded brusquely. "Going for a stone," he muttered and moved toward the outside staircase.

When Judy and Dantan and Miri and Seymour had completed their descent Miri said, "There's a laundry up the hill, a mother and two daughters. Some of the foreigners take their wash there. It's interesting, you should go have a look. They use cast-iron irons that have to be heated on the coal-stove."

Judy said, "Where can I buy a couple? They sound like they would make good bookends."

Miri smiled at her friend's unwavering focus. "Some of the foreigners use this laundry, the ones who don't have their maids do their wash for them. Francine told me that Hugo used to have his done at the *fonda* until he came upon a couple of the maids holding up a pair of his enormous baggy pants and laughing.

"And Jorgen?" Dantan asked. "Was he going to collect his laundry in that empty sack?"

"He was probably going to collect a piece of pink sandstone from the fields, to carve something. He's good."

"Should I buy one of his works?" Judy asked.

"My wife is by way of being an art-collector," Dantan told Seymour. His smile conveyed that he didn't take it very seriously.

"I'll take you to his studio before you leave. It's in the basement here at the *fonda*. But I don't know if any of his pieces are available for sale. He has a financial arrangement with a band of Stockholm dentists who send him a monthly allowance, and then expect to get a piece of his work after some specified amount of time. He's always behind in his commitments so he may not want to part with anything to anyone else."

Now Judy was really interested, and insisted that Miri arrange for her to see his work.

Judy's faithful taxi-driver was waiting for them, they all climbed into the cab and rumbled forth half-way around the bay to Hotel Palma Linda. Miri pointed out to Seymour that if they kept on going past the hotel, round the bay, they would arrive at her house.

"Am I going to get to see it?" Seymour smiled.

"If you want," Miri said nonchalantly. She would have been disappointed if he had not wanted to.

"Alphie and I will come too," Judy said brightly, with a look at Dantan, who nodded. "I've been wanting to see it. We can all go in the taxi."

Dantan smiled. "The old driver is ecstatic over the amount of business Judy has been giving him, more than he makes in a year. He's planning on buying a new set of used tires, less bald than the ones he has been rattling around on for years."

As the waiter set up a beautiful table for them in the suite, laying a colorful hand-embroidered linen cloth preparatory to serving a sumptuous lunch, Miri brought Seymour up to date on the murder, and the fact of Tomas' disappearance after the body had been discovered and he had been warned by Max and Fred and Catalina that the *Guardia Civil* were looking to arrest him for the murder. "It's amazing that he just turned up like that, four or five days later, nonchalantly showing his face."

"Yes," Dantan said, "when I spoke with him at the dock he seemed very calm, made an appointment with me to get together at a local *bodega* this evening."

"Maybe the police have arrested someone else," Judy said hopefully.

"We would have heard about it," Miri assured her. "When one person in this crowd hears anything, it spreads to everyone else like wildfire."

Seymour, having been apprised of all the facts known so far, observed, "The simplest explanation for the girl's body being found by Tomas' truck was that he killed her himself."

Dantan nodded. "I'm inclined to think that too, except that if he had, why did he carry her to the doctor's? He could have just left her body on the dock, then driven off to the city as he had planned."

After a delicious meal the four of them piled into "Judy's" taxi and drove off on the bumpy dirt road to Miri's house.

The visitors were all duly astonished by the beautiful view of the bay and beyond, the village waterfront. Scrubby pines on the shore near Miri's house framed the picture.

Judy asked, "Have you done a painting of this?"

"Not yet." Miri had no intention of painting any more "travel posters".

They went inside. The visitors were surprised at how cool it was.

"Built of thick concrete blocks, and cleverly designed so that the sun never shines directly in," explained Miri.

After briefly inspecting the kitchen, with its red tile counter and small cabinet and coal stove, about which Judy only said, "You cook in *this*?" they all tropped into the main room. This was large, with excellent north light.

Miri's paintings were standing against the walls, painting-side in. She turned them out, one by one. Judy liked the "travel posters." The portrait of Teresa, sitting by her hearth, and of the dying child lying in her bed, were too sad for Judy's taste. No use telling her they were better paintings.

The Dantans refused refreshment, they had had too much already, and as Miri had no ice-box any cold drinks would not be cold.

"You two go on ahead without me," Seymour grinned at Judy and Dantan. "I'll hang around here for awhile, and then walk back."

Judy giggled, and made sure she and her husband departed quickly.

Seymour put his arms around Miri, holding her tight and kissing her all over. "Come back to the States with me, and we'll get married."

"I told you before. I'm going to be an artist."

"Fine. Can't you be an artist in Queens? At least until I start making enough money to move anywhere you want as long as it's close enough to my job."

There were advantages to this if she could admit it. Seymour smelled nice. And felt good. And he was crazy enough to love her without seeming crazy otherwise. Furthermore, though she wouldn't admit it for the world, she was bored out of her mind in San Marino. And it was too hot.

She said, "No."

Seymour grinned. "Somehow I don't believe you. So I'll be checking with you again soon."

They went to bed. It wasn't as large or as comfortable as the big bed Seymour had had in Paris, but it was still good.

Back at their rooms at the Hotel Palma Linda, Judy was reluctant to go out again. It was nice and cool in their rooms, and so hot outside, and she didn't feel like meeting up with the oddballs yet again. She knew that Miri would be preoccupied with Seymour for awhile, so they couldn't go shopping together just yet.

Dantan was just as satisfied to remain within, to think over the "case."

Now that he had met the Belge and the Great Dane, he realized he would have to question them thoroughly as soon as possible. Both resided where the dead girl had worked, and both were used to being seen carrying large sacks around, so if the body were in one of them it would not be especially noted.

He very badly needed a medical estimate of when the killing could have occurred. Maria's body was found by Tomas very early Monday morning, before seven. Dantan went over his mind what he had learned so far from his conversations with the expatriates and the Ibizans. As far as he had been able to ascertain, the last time anyone had seen the girl alive was some time Sunday evening, but no one he had spoken to yet had been able to pinpoint the time. Maria had been collecting dirty clothes that guests had wanted laundered. Francine had seen Maria picking up a bundle at one of the guests' doors, but couldn't remember which one.

Ilse was the first to notice Maria's absence Monday morning, when Maria did not show up for work. She questioned Consuelo, who could shed no light on the question. She herself had been so exhausted when she got home from work that night, that she had fallen onto her little bed and fallen asleep immediately. If she thought about her sister at all, she probably thought Maria, who had not had to work Sunday night, was still socializing after the movie.

Dantan thought about the staff at the *fonda*. Almost all of them were young girls, one of them Maria's own sister. Somehow, he just couldn't see any of them as a killer.

He had already ruled out the coal-stoker because he was so permeated with fine coal-dust that he couldn't possibly have laid a hand on anyone without leaving some coal-dust behind. So too, for

his cart in which he hauled coal from the coal-
dealer's. As for Ilse, having met her, tough bird
though she was, Dantan firmly believed she was too
focused on her business to do anything that would
jeopardize it. He would have to look elsewhere for
his murderer.

ELEVEN

A QUIET RETURN

The bar Tomas had selected as a meeting place was in San Marino, on the same street as the butcher's shop. The bar was crowded with Ibizan workmen. No one noticed Tomas, or if they did, were not letting on. The two men sat at a table in the back and sized up each other. Dantan saw an open honest face before him. Some of the more successful con-men had such open honest faces. So did some honest men. Dantan did not think he was clever enough to tell the difference.

"My sister told me about you," Tomas said. "She said the foreigners asked you to help find the person who actually killed poor Maria."

Dantan nodded. "But I am here as a tourist, with my wife. She has an American friend who came to San Marino to paint, and we came principally to visit her. I said I would do what I could, unofficially, to help, without offending the attention of the local authorities."

The two men conversed in the language that they had in common, English. Tomas' English was impeccable. This was another sort of Ibicencan than Dantan had met so far. Tomas was self-assured, prosperous, educated.

"I can't contribute anything to that search," Tomas said, "but I can explain to you where I have been, and why, as it would not be surprising if you suspected me of the killing."

Dantan gestured for him to continue.

"When I found Maria lying beside my truck I honestly did not know that she was dead. I thought she was unconscious, I didn't know why. I didn't waste time trying to figure out what she was doing there, but picked her up, put her in my truck and drove off in a hurry to the doctor.

"I left her in the care of the doctor's maid, and drove off to go about my business in the city of Ibiza. One of my stops was at a *tienda* owned by an uncle where I was to take a small order from him. My cousin Inez was alone there, tending shop. Soon after I arrived, one of the San Marino taxis rattled up. It was carrying my sister and three of the foreigners who lived in San Marino, looking for me.

"Catalina was very agitated. She said that the *Guardia Civil* were looking for me. Maria was dead. The doctor had reported to them that she had been strangled. The *Guardia Civil* seemed to think I had killed Maria. Catalina was frightened for me, sure I would be emprisoned immediately, without further investigation to find out who had really done the murder. She urged me to go somewhere and hide, perhaps with one of our relatives in town.

"I couldn't bring myself to actually hide, but I did think it prudent to stay out of the reach of the police until matters might be clarified."

Dantan marvelled at the precision which could distinguish between "couldn't bring myself to hide" and "prudent to stay out of reach."

Tomas went on, "I gave Inez the keys to my truck so that she could give them to her brother, who was coming later to help in the *tienda.* He would park it somewhere out of sight.

"I refused to take the offer of a ride in the taxi Catalina and the foreigners had arrived in – they were going right back to San Marino – and walked into Ibiza, where I spent the rest of the day walking up and down the streets. At dusk, I went to my uncle's house. He was, as usual, inebriated, but he had learned what had happened and assured me that his son had safely left the truck somewhere where it was unlikely to be seen by the police. I left my uncle's home at dawn, in case any police should come looking for me there, and wandered around until it was time for the Tuesday boat to leave for Barcelona.

"In Barcelona, I lingered over coffee at a bar until the shops opened. Then I bought myself shaving equipment, some clean underwear, a clean shirt, and a small suitcase. I changed into my new clothes in a public lavatory. I then took a room in a boarding-house in the heart of the city. I filled out the papers honestly, showed my identity card, and could only pray that the inefficient bureaucracy would not have the time to trace me before I was off again.

"After washing up and shaving, I went to the offices of the most important man my father knew in Barcelona, a very successful merchant. He listened to my story and agreed to help. I stayed in his offices until he was able to contact his lawyer and had explained the situation to him. They worked out a plan to create the chain of contacts that could be bribed to keep the local police in San Marino away from me. The merchant would advance the money needed and was taking it on faith that my father would repay him.

"That was Wednesday. Their calls and promises did not take long. Money travels faster than man himself can. Last night, by the time the Friday boat was to leave Barcelona for Ibiza, I was assured that it would be safe for me to board for home. This morning I retrieved my truck from my uncle, and drove back to San Marino."

"So you feel it is safe for you here in San Marino now?"

"I am sure of it, for the moment. But I don't know how long the chain will hold, how much it will cost to keep it holding. And it doesn't mean that the authorities do not still think I murdered the girl, only that they are not going to touch me for it – for awhile. As more time elapses, there will no doubt be expectations for greater bribes, and it is not tenable that our family continue in that way indefinitely. However, at least for now I can help with the family business again, and do whatever I can to assist in investigations to find the killer and clear me. Obviously, if the police were to discover evidence implicating me in the crime, they would probably arrest me even if it cost them their bribe money. But they won't. I did nothing wrong."

"Thank you for telling me all this," said Dantan, knowing he would have to mull it over by himself to see how much he believed.

"Are you going to stay in San Marino now?"

"Yes, but I will try to remain discreetly out of sight, helping at my father's store only in back, until I have the right moment to speak with the local police and make sure they are fixed. If I sense any hesitation, or of course, overt agression, I plan on disappearing again, to another town. I hope I don't have to do that. I hope you can help us."

"I hope so too," said Dantan, still uncertain whether his help was warranted.

TWELVE

PASEO

Sunday morning there was a funeral mass for Maria. It was attended by all the Ibizans of San Marino (except those who had to work). The mourners joined Maria's mother and sister Consuelo, and two brothers who lived and worked in Ibiza city and had come in by bus the night before, and Maria's girlfriends, and fellow workers from the *fonda*.

The only foreigners who attended were Hans and Ilse, and Francine, who was Catholic and often attended Sunday Mass anyway. The other foreigners pursued their usual activities, sleeping off the drinking of the night before or gathering at Liberto's cafe to begin a new round.

By the time Dantan and Judy, in a pale green sleeveless linen sheath and green sandals, arrived in the village, a group had already gathered at Liberto's cafe. Nigel signalled Liberto to place two chairs for Dantan and Judy between himself and Pamela, and he immediately began questioning Dantan in a friendly way about his progress.

Besides Nigel and Pamela, Lady Mary, Max, Harriet, Lotte and Leo were there. Hugo pulled up on his Vespa soon after, parking by the palm tree near the foreigners' table. Harriet greeted him but the others ignored him. He pulled up a chair beside Harriet. Liberto placed a hot chocolate before him, and a pile of sweet rolls. He began stuffing a roll into his mouth and slurping his beverage.

Dantan had no intention of mentioning his meeting with Tomas. It might be inevitable that the winds of gossip would relay to this crowd that Tomas had reappeared, but Dantan would not be the one to reveal it. Nigel had to be satisfied with Dantan's calm response: "I've been thinking about it."

Max had come up with an ingenious theory. "I've come to the conclusion that members of the *Guardia Civil* killed the girl, because a murder investigation would make them seem more important, and they blamed Tomas Bonet because he is the most enviable of all the San Marino men. His father owns a lucrative business, and is considered rich by local standards, Tomas himself has had a quality education in Barcelona and if he so chose, could leave the island for a more interesting profitable life on the mainland. He is also extremely handsome and is taller than any of the Ibizan men." Max grinned widely, and looked around for responses to his theory.

"Spoken like a true fiction-writer!" Nigel laughed. "It has the makings of a plot for one of your novels."

"It's quite logical," Max said, somewhat deflated.

Harriet unexpectantly rose to Max' defense. "Why, it makes a lot of sense! All the other Ibizans are so sweet they couldn't possibly have done it!"

"Well, what about one of us?" Nigel asked.

"Nonsense," said Lady Mary, with only a slight slur. "We're all quite civilized."

"Here comes someone who is not entirely civilized," grinned Max as Jorgen strode over.

The giant pulled a chair from another table and sat down beside Judy Dantan. "Madame. You have the beauty of a Rubens. I would like to do a sculpture of you."

Judy blushed deeply and before she could speak, Dantan told Jorgen pleasantly, "We'll be leaving in a few days, there isn't time. Thanks for the compliment anyway." He put his arm around his wife possessively. "I think she is beautiful too."

"My friend Miri told me you're a good sculptor," Judy said, recovering her composure. "May we get to look at some of your work?"

His wife, always on the lookout for additions to her art collection, had played right into Dantan's wish to ask Herr Jorgen a few more questions – without seeming to be in his guise of detective.

"Your friend Miri has a good head. I would like to do it in stone."

This was not exactly an invitation to see his studio again, but Dantan was satisfied to leave it to his wife and her friend to manage one.

"Where is the Round Square this morning?" Max asked, looking around.

"The Round Square?" Judy asked.

"That's what Max calls your friend Miri," Pamela laughed with a little trill. "He has names for all of us, not very attractive ones, but we tolerate our own because the others are often amusing."

"A boyfriend of hers arrived yesterday," Judy said.

"She has a boyfriend?" Max said with mock surprise. "I would have bet money that she is a virgin."

"The two are not mutually exclusive," Lady Mary majestically declared.

Earlier that morning Seymour had hiked to Miri's house, bearing fresh *enpanadillas* and a big thermos he had purchased at the Bonets' general store, and then had filled with strong steaming coffee with hot milk from Liberto's. Also from Liberto's he brought four hard-boiled eggs. He didn't want Miri to trouble starting up the coal-stove.

As Miri had no movable seating, Seymour carried one of the straw mattresses from the guest-room onto the front patio overlooking the bay, where they had breakfast. "I would buy you a couple of chairs," he grinned, "except that I'm hoping you'll leave this place with me soon."

"Don't spend your money on any chairs," Miri smiled, then added hastily, "That doesn't mean I'm going anywhere with you." But she surely did like being with him.

"You don't have to stay until your money runs out, you know. It's so damn hot here."

"This house is cool."

"Well if you do stay until your money runs out, and I hope you set aside enough for the boat trip home, what will you do then?"

"I have no idea. I'm just trying to do some good paintings and not think beyond that." Fine words, but she recognized uncomfortably that she had hardly done any good paintings.

Seymour put his arm around her. "Want to go to the movies tonight? We could neck in the back row."

Miri laughed. "There is no back row. Everybody moves their chairs around whenever someone else moves, or jumps up and knocks a chair over. I don't know what's playing."

"There's a flamboyant poster for it at the *fonda*, Charlton Heston in full cowboy regalia galloping on his horse. It's called 'Pony Express.' The poster was not in Spanish."

"You can be sure it will be dubbed, though. They can't have subtitles, most of this audience can't read, and anyway, the Spanish censors have to make sure not a trace of sex or irreverence or ungodliness or criticism of Franco gets through. The crowd will be whooping it up for a Western. We'll have to buy at least two bars of chocolate to get through it."

Sunday evening the two couples were going to meet to watch the *paseo* when the young girls of the village, dressed in long silk or satin dresses, strolled slowly and gracefully around the village square. They were heavily adorned with masses of beads and bangles, whatever their families could afford. These were signals of the dowry that could be expected. The young men also ambled around the square, inspecting the girls.

Because unmarried Ibizan girls were attended by chaperones, each of Dantan's interviews with the maids of the *fonda* was accompanied by the same old woman, an aunt of Maria's and Consuelo's. She spoke only Ibicencan. Catalina was also there to interpret. Every question of Dantan's had to be translated into Ibicencan and every reply from each of the girls translated from Ibicencan into English. Dantan was impressed by Catalina's intelligence, and her ability speak English so well. "My brother has taught me everything," she said simply. "I only went to the small children's class with the nuns."

Dantan asked the same questions of each girl: "Do you remember when was the last time you saw Maria? Where? Did she say anything to you?"

Maria had been seen the previous Sunday going about her regular late morning work of making the beds and cleaning the guests' rooms. At midday she worked in the kitchen, helping serve the midday meal, and was seen by all the others there. She was last seen, soon after the midday meal was cleared, going down to the basement to do laundry. There was always loads of *fonda* laundry — sheets and towels and tablecloths and napkins — but in addition, guests could get their personal laundry done for an extra charge. That Sunday there had been no other maids working in the laundry besides Maria.

Nobody remembered seeing her at the *paseo* or afterwards, at the Sunday movie. Her sister Consuelo, who was being courted by three young men, had remained at her family's home to be called on by each of them in turn. In any event, Maria had a servants' room at the *fonda* and would often stay there overnight, as her family's house was over-crowded even without her. With Consuelo's suitors, and the other Sunday night activities, nobody at home missed Maria.

Dantan hoped to speak with the coal-stoker, who may have been working on the furnace while Maria was scrubbing laundry. And Jorgen had al-ready told Dantan that he had been working in his studio in the basement and seen Maria down there. Or more than just seen her?

Dantan also wanted to question Ilse and Hans and the other guests at the *fonda*. He hoped to ac-complish all this on Monday.

One crucial conversation which Dantan needed to have was with Consuelo, or rather, with Catalina who would explain everything to Consuelo, related to collecting evidence.

He had already told Catalina what he wanted Consuelo to do, providing she could be unobserved. He emphasized that Consuelo should take no risks at all. Dantan had already provided Catalina with several things he wanted put into Consuelo's hands, and she now handed them, tied up in a scarf, to Consuelo. The scarf contained Judy's nail-scissors, her tweezers, a packet of already-numbered glassine envelopes secured with a rubber-band, and a blue wax pencil. Catalina instructed Consuelo to snip inconspicuous samples from the bedding and clothing of each of the guests whose rooms she cleaned, making sure to keep straight which was which. As she didn't know how to write, she was to use whatever marks made sense to her, to tell them apart.

Consuelo was very eager to help. She wanted to help avenge her sister, and she was excited at a challenging task. Catalina communicated her response, and Dantan could observe her enthusiasm. He was sure that Consuelo would have loved learning to read and write, and would have done well at her studies. She smiled shyly, saying, "*gracias, Señor,*" over and over as if he had conferred an immense favor on her.

Suddenly Consuelo started chattering to Catalina in a more excited tone. Catalina translated: "Consuelo just remembered something that Maria told her not long ago. She wonders if it is important. Maria was cleaning the house of *Senor* Max while *Señorita* Francine the French girl, was still living there. They got into a loud argument and suddenly he was hitting her. Maria was in another room but could see through the doorway. *Señor* Max grabbed *Señorita* Francine by the arm and dragged her to the doorway to the house, tossed her like garbage onto the ground, then grabbed up an armful of her clothing and threw that outside too. Maria was terrified and hid for awhile until *Señor* Max went out. When she left, *Señorita* Francine was nowhere to be seen."

Dantan thanked both girls for their help.

What Consuelo now told him was consistent with the gossip that he had heard about Max, and his brutal treatment of Francine, but the one added fact was that Maria had seen an example of it firsthand. As a witness was she a threat to him? It seemed far-fetched, but that was because he lacked adequate facts.

THIRTEEN

TWIT &TWERP

The first order of the day on Monday was to spek to the doctor. Dantan had learned that his office hours were ten o'clock to noon. That was it. The rest of the day was reserved for operations, such as appendectomies. (The doctor continued to have patients among the peasons for appendectomies despite the persistent rumor, at least among the foreigners, that many of the operations were the result of an incorrect diagnosis, and that one patient in three died.)

Miri would have to go over to the cat-owners quite early. Dantan hoped that they would be in, and receptive to a morning visit. Miri felt extreme discomfort at the thought of just dropping in but realized her sneezing might be helpful as an entree to the doctor.

Judy came up with a clever ruse for visiting the two men which couldn't be a purely social visit since Miri, like many of the others, disliked the two men and would not have voluntarily "dropped in." But Judy, after gossiping with Harriet (who although always careful to try to say kind things about everyone, was nevertheless aware of everyone's quirks and foibles and was not averse to imparting them — in gentle terms), learned that Twit and Twerp were very house-proud. They had decorated their home with things from their jaunts to North Africa and Portugal. This would give her and Miri an excuse for calling on them.

Judy and Miri showed up at ten Monday morning and brightly asked if it was convenient to see their house. "I've heard so much about it," Judy gushed, "that I was really hoping you would let us take a peek. I'm still decorating my apartment in Paris, and from what I heard, I might get some inspiring ideas from you two."

Percy, especially, was overwhelmed by Judy's effusive flattery, and ushered them right in. The two men had been sitting around over the remains of breakfast, smoking English cigarettes, and sipping champagne. A half-empty bottle sat on the table.

They seemed pleased to be caught in the act of drinking champagne for breakfast. Percy offered some to the two visitors and Edgar bustled off to the kitchen for two more champagne glasses, before Judy or Miri could say no.

The little house was definitely "decorated"! Flowered prints and ruffles dominated the scene, colorful pottery was crammed onto every shelf and table, and on the floor huge copper pieces whose function had been lost in time held huge ugly cacti.

"I'd love to know where each of your beautiful things came from," Judy bubbled. "So I can track things down and copy you!"

Percy was only too happy to oblige, and began a detailed narration of their possessions. The colorful handpainted tiles that adorned the kitchen walls were from Portugal, as were pieces of pottery on a shelf over the fireplace. Ruffled linen in an overall design of large rose and blue flowers covered fat cushions that sat like dowagers on otherwise austere rattan chairs. The cushion fabric had been sent from England. The handwoven rug of an intricate design in brilliant blues was from Morocco, as were some brass pitchers on another table. During Percy's disquisition, the girls were gratified to note, the three cats had rather judiciously appeared and were checking out their legs. One after the other, the furry creatures rubbed up against the women, winding in and out of their legs and the table. One of the cats, the gray one, actually leapt up into Miri's lap!

"Marilyn likes you!" Edgar said ecstatically, clapping his hands.

Miri began petting Marilyn gingerly, and was rewarded with constant ecstatic purring. Miri felt a sudden urge to sneeze, but by sheer will-power managed to suppress it. A second urge, a little later, burst out explosively. She apologized. Nobody seemed to care. The cat, startled by the explosive sound, jumped down from Miri's lap, but when the sneezing subsided, she jumped back up.

Then the black cat, a large fat thing, joined Marilyn in Miri's lap!

"Beezlebub too!" Edgar rejoiced, as if he were in heaven. Miri, who was now sneezing violently and often, wondered at the ways of nature that a cat-hater should get such affection from two felines. Even the third cat, a fat white one with big orange spots whom Twit and Twerp affectionately called "Marlene", while not trying to join her fellows in her lap, persisted in continually rubbing against her legs.

As soon as politely possible, and after swallowing their champagne quickly, Miri and Judy took their leave. Meeting with Dantan, they raced off to the doctor's office. It was twenty past eleven. Miri was still sneezing violently.

The doctor had an impressive house high on a hill. It was the only one in town with real grass, an incredible luxury in an area where water was scarce.

He had a special cistern to store water just for his lawn.

The doctor's waiting-room was decorated with heavy Spanish antique furniture and various colorful banners.

"I love these chairs!" Judy whispered. "I wonder where I could get some like them?"

"Don't we already have enough uncomfortable chairs?" her husband asked drily.

In one of the big mahogany chairs a little boy was crouched, looking pained, holding his foot, which was stuck all over with conch needles, on his knee.

Miri and her friends were hoping that the sneezing wouldn't wear off by the time the doctor finished removing all the child's conch needles.

They needn't have worried. The maid came to tell them the doctor would see them. When they indicated the child, she shrugged. "He can wait."

The doctor's office had Art Deco furnishings trimmed in chrome. He sat Miri down in an examining-chair and began peering into her nose and ears with a little flashlight and then into her throat with a wooden tongue-depressor, on which she gagged. The sneezing had kicked in satisfactorily, and the doctor cringed at each sneeze, as if he were afraid of catching whatever she had.

The doctor spoke quite passable English, although with a heavy Spanish accent. Miri was happy that she wouldn't have to struggle with her rudimentary Spanish between sneezes.

Judy kept up a continuous line of chatter as if they were there on a social call. She flattered the doctor "as one of the few highly educated persons in the village and a pleasure to talk with," and by the time he had pronounced the diagnosis that Miri had the flu, based on what he had seen in Miri's ears, nose and throat, Judy was able to ask him casually, "Wasn't that terrible what happened to the poor young maid at the *fonda*? Your opinion of what might have happened would be most respected."

"A beast strangled her."

"But who could have done such a horrible thing?" Judy sighed.

"Oh, Tomas Bonet, without a doubt. He strangled her, then brought her here to give himself an alibi."

"How long had she been deceased when he brought her here?" Dantan ventured to ask.

"What difference does that make? She was dead."

He fetched a large glass jar containing a white powder from one of his handsome cabinets, then spooned a quantity into a large envelope. He handed this to Miri, with instructions to mix a tablespoon of the powder in tea every four hours.

"For how long?" Miri asked, but the doctor had already disappeared into another room and closed the door.

"Until dead," Judy giggled.

"He didn't say anything about taking the medicine," Dantan chuckled, "only to mix it in tea."

"You are so logical, Alphie," Judy said affectionately.

Miri was surprised to hear that her empty-headed friend had noticed that her husband was logical, and appreciated it. Maybe she had underrated Judy?

"Let's hope he was as wrong about Tomas as he was about Miri's flu," Dantan said wryly. "He seems to have exercised no intellectual curiosity about the death."

A secretary was now seated at her desk near the door. Dantan paid the doctor's bill, with an additional sum for the unnamed white powder. The bill was not small, for San Marino. Dantan supposed that they were charged more because they were foreigners. But at least they didn't have to take the doctor's advice or his medicine.

The secretary helped the boy in the waiting-room hop into the doctor's office, numerous conch-needles dangling from the bare foot he held in the air.

Dantan and Judy and Miri were to join Seymour for *comida* at the *Fonda Bahia.* This would afford Dantan an opportunity to engage in a discussion of the murder, and raise questions to those of the guests who might appear. He had hopes that many or all of them would be there, as the midday meal was going to be *paella,* very popular with all.

The crowded *fonda* dining-room was bustling. Three long tables of eight seats each were filling up quickly, one with a group of Spanish tourists, another with Germans. Ilse came out of the kitchen to welcome *Senor* Levin's guests. She made sure to seat them with her longer-term foreigners: Jorgen, Hugo, Francine, and Claude.

One of the maids carried in a large heavy tureen of soup, and proceeded to ladle into each of their plates a steaming portion of thick tomato brew.

Jorgen said to Miri, as he had several times before, "I would like to do your head."

"And," Judy whispered to Miri, giggling, "he would like to do my body!"

Miri said to him, "I think my friends here would like to see your work."

Jorgen nodded absently. He was staring at Miri's head as if he were already planning out his sculpture.

"You work long hours?" Dantan asked him.

"I work when I feel inspiration. That could be what you call long hours."

Miri envied him for that. But of course he was much older than she was, by at least ten years, and had been practicing art much longer than she had.

They all spooned their soup in silence for a short while, then the maid cleared the plates and carried in an enormous platter piled high with steaming *paella.* She placed the platter before Judy.

Miri wondered how a skinny girl like that could carry such a heavy dish. Dantan was noting the same thing. Someone strong enough to carry that weight might be strong enough to strangle a thin frail girl.

For the *paella* they were left on their own to dish out what they wanted. Judy presided, dumping lavish portions on each of the plates as they were passed to her, making sure everyone got chicken, clams, *chorizo*, in equal measure, along with the steaming saffron rice.

Although Seymour almost never took his eyes off Miri, giving her smiles and squeezing her hand under the table, he managed to put away a surprising quantity of *paella*. He was the first to accept seconds, followed closely by the Belge.

Claude said appreciately, "This is a superb dish. Too bad they don't cook like this all the time. When I have my restaurant I shall certainly offer a Spanish dish or two if it can be made as delicious as this."

"Pedro's has good *paella*," said Francine in a wispy voice, in French to Claude.

"Really? I didn't know you had ever been there."

"Max took me there once."

Claude stared at the discolored skin around one of her eyes. "I see you are still seeing him," he said sardonically.

Francine dropped her head.

Dantan had still not exchanged any conversation with the Belge, who was shoveling *paella* into his face at a rate that suggested he expected an imminent worldwide famine. Dantan asked him pleasantly. "Have you been staying here long?"

"Since last December."

"How is the winter here?" Miri asked.

"Cool but not cold. It rains incessantly all of February. Only time of year it does rain. That's their only chance to get the cisterns filled up."

"But you've stayed."

"Oh, I go to Palma or Paris now and then," he said loftily. "Or my cocoa plantation in the Congo."

"So you must know everyone here pretty well," Dantan remarked, ignoring the mention of a cocoa plantation, which was probably one of Hugo's well-known lies. "The locals, I mean."

"I don't have much to do with the locals," the Belge said disdainfully.

"Some of the local girls are very pretty," Judy smiled.

The Belge blushed a deep red, from his neck up to his ears.

Judy asked boldly, "Have you ever dated any of them?"

Hugo now buried his face in his food.

Francine, who had pushed around the food on her plate and had actually eaten very little, now got up. "I'm not having any *postre*." She left.

"She should have stayed until it was served her, then one of us could have had her portion," Hugo grumbled.

But he got it anyway. The maid bringing in the individual portions of pudding, seeing that she had an extra one, placed it before Jorgen with a shy smile. Jorgen immediately passed it over to Hugo. This was the first hint Judy had seen that there might be any romance between any of these lugubrious foreigners and a local girl. She loved match-making. She also kept on eye on Seymour and Miri, and could see that he was still smitten with her, but she was being her usual nutty self.

After the meal Dantan, Judy and Miri followed Jorgen down to his studio in the basement. Seymour said he was going to wander around.

On a worktable were pieces ranging from one to three or four feet high. All were abstractions of the human form. None of them appeared to Miri to be completed. It seemed that Jorgen liked to have a number of projects going at once.

Judy whispered to Miri, "I don't see what good it would do him to work from your head or my body. These don't really look like people."

"You don't have to like them," Jorgen said in a loud voice from across the room where he was talking with Dantan. "I don't care what people who don't know anything about art think."

Judy spoke up boldly: "What about people who don't know anything about art who do like your work?"

Miri smiled at her friend, who seemed to be developing a more assertive personality.

Dantan wondered if there were anything else he could ask Jorgen that he had not already. He could think of nothing.

FOURTEEN

MATANZA

Monday afternoon Judy felt the need for a *siesta*, a custom she was seriously thinking of instituting back in Paris too. She and Dantan returned to their hotel in what had become her personal transportation – the ancient black taxi.. Seymour and Miri retreated to the latter's house on foot.

Dantan was anxious to see what Consuelo had been able to obtain in the way of possible evidence, but he was unsure where to look for her, and when. He had hoped to encounter her at the meal at the *fonda*, but had not done so. After his contribution to the *siesta* was concluded, he trudged back into the village, prepared to wait at Liberto's until someone turned up who could guide him to Consuelo, at least for a progress report.

Mavis was the solitary figure under the Cinzano umbrella, looking downcast. "How goes it?" Dantan asked her.

She gave him a wan smile. "I don't know what to do," she sighed. "I am morose."

"I'm listening."

"I feel at peace here, and I would like to settle here, but I'm afraid that by the time I go through all the effort of having a house built, San Marino will have changed. And Vicente. I would like to marry him and live with him always. He is a truly good and honest soul and he is the sexiest man I've ever known. But I couldn't even say 'I do' in his language or he in mine!"

"The changes to San Marino that may occur, you can't do much about. But the language problem you can. Learn Ibicencan. You could pay Catalina to teach you. Her English is excellent and she is a charming person."

"I think I'm too lazy."

There was no answer to that! That might be a truth, moreover, that could apply to many of the foreigners living here for extended stays.

Mavis, or any of the others, had not said a word about knowing that Tomas Bonet was back in San Marino. He thought it possible that he was the only foreigner who knew. He was concerned about what the *Guardia Civil* would do when they learned Tomas was here, despite Tomas' strong confidence that the police had been "fixed." There seemed no local investigations going on into an alternate suspect.

""What time does the Bonet store re-open after the *siesta*?" he asked Mavis disingenuously. "I need shaving cream."

"Oh it's open already, they close only for a short siesta. Not like the rest of the places. The post-office, for instance, doesn't open until after five."

Dantan walked off in the direction of the Bonets' general store.

Catalina was at the counter. No one else was in the shop. She produced the tube of Spanish shaving cream he requested, and giving him his change, murmured that Consuelo had something for him. Best if he just waited here, while she fetched Consuelo.

This took only a few minutes. Maria's sister arrived with a number of items tied up in a scarf, handed the bundle to Dantan and waited while he looked inside. He saw a number of glassine envelopes with a variety of marks in blue wax pencil, as well as the nail-scissors and the tweezers. He passed the envelopes to Catalina as Consuelo rattled off to Catalina, scribbling rapidly, what the marks signified.

Catalina wrote out the names of the *fonda* guests from which Consuelo had retrieved her samples, and beside the names she wrote the numbers of the coresponding glassine envelopes.

She gave Dantan a paper bag large enough to hold the scarf and its contents and the shaving-cream, thriftily taking back the smaller bag she had first put the shaving-cream in.

"Tomas said to tell you 'hello'," she smiled. "He's in Ibiza city with one of our uncles, and helping him with his business. Avoids the local gossip here."

Dantan was grateful for the information.

He trudged back to their hotel, where he found his wife awake but lolling in bed, eating a persimmon.

"I want to write to Jean-Jacques," he told her.

""Then I'll do whatever you wish."

"I'm happy right here. It's too hot to go out yet."

Dantan sat down at their writing-table, well equipped with hotel stationery. He took all the glassine envelopes he had collected from the body at the ice-house and added them to the pile of those Consuelo had provided, and proceeded to document for Jean-Jacques just what he was sending him for forensic analysis. They had arranged before the

Dantans' departure that Dantan would mail any such materials to Jean-Jacques at his rooms to avoid any Spanish snoops from noticing mail going to the Paris *Police Judiciare*. When he had results he would telephone Dantan at the Hotel Palma Linda, from Dantan's own apartment. Germaine had been told to expect the visit, and his use of the telephone.

Consuelo had collected snippets from blankets in the rooms of Jorgen, Claude, Hugo, Francine, and three other tourists with the Spanish party. From these same guests she taken small pieces of fabric from the seams of two garments each. She had also included threads from two gray sacks, one from Jorgen's room, and one from Hugo's. Dantan recalled seeing the two men using these sacks, the Belge to transport his laundry, Jorgen to carry stones back to his studio.

Consuelo had done a professional well-organized job. And this from a fifteen-year-old who couldn't read or write. Just think of what she could have accomplished had she been literate!

The letter to Jean-Jacques completed, Dantan placed it and the glassine envelopes in a hotel envelope, wrote his own name and suite-number with a flourish on the return address and sealed it up. It was maddening to think that his letter would not begin its journey to Paris until Tuesday evening

when the mailbags from San Marino would be transported onto the boat in Ibiza departing for Mallorca
and arriving there Wednesday morning, to then be
put aboard a plane to Paris.

By five, his wife had arisen, taken a soothing
bath and dressed in another of her new dresses, this
one light blue, and matching light blue sandals.

The Dantans climbed into their taxi which
rattled off down the dirt road, barely missing two
chickens and a dog which Dantan suspected that the
driver had aimed at on purpose.

"Miri told me a secret she's ashamed to tell
you, but it's been bothering her that it might influ-
ence your thinking about who killed the girl."

"Did Miri tell you not to tell me?"

Judy admitted that she had.

"Much as I would like every shred of information I can get, I don't like you telling someone's
secret if they told you not to. So please do not. I'll
try very hard to solve this case without it." Dantan
knew it was hopeless to keep his wife from telling
secrets that had been confided to her but in this instance, especially, he would wager that Miri's secret
was some embarassing encounter she had had with
one of the men here, which had stimulated her over-
active imagination. He could do without it, and save
his wife's honor too! Although in all honesty, he had

to admit to himself that if this were a "real" case, a case he had to solve at the Paris *Police Judiciare*, he would have accepted the information about Miri's secret, any scrap that might advance his investigation.

Miri and the others were at the cafe. She waved to them excitedly. Dantan wondered if she was going to tell him her "secret" after all. But no. She wanted to tell him that her maid Teresa had told her that Consuelo told her that Maria had told her that she was in love with Tomas! Wasn't that suggestive? That she may have chased after him and he went farther than she expected and she resisted and threatened to tell on him and the worst happened....

Dantan said he would think about it in the context of everything else he had gleaned so far.

Then Miri, with great enthusiasm, switched to a totally different topic. "I've been invited to Teresa's family's *matanza*! I tried to get Seymour and you two invited too but Teresa said it is usually just relatives and inviting me was a special honor. I'll fit in because I look Spanish, and there are so many cousins probably very few will notice."

"What's a *matanza*?" Judy asked.

"They slaughter a pig they've been fattening up all year, and drink the blood and have a feast and make sausages and ham to put by to eat the rest of the year. It's just about the only meat they get to eat all year, they can't afford to buy any."

"Ugh! And you're going to that?"

"It's local color. And foreigners don't usually get to see it."

"If that's local color I'll take black and white," giggled Judy. "Are you really going?"

"I told Teresa I would."

"Well, you know those little bags they put near your seat on airplanes – puke-pockets – be sure to take along a couple."

"Who actually does the slaughtering?" Dantan asked.

"I don't know. Some of the men in the family, I guess."

Dantan didn't want to make Miri self-conscious in advance, but he was going to ask her after it was over who had done the butchering. After all, it took a certain *sang-froid* to slaughter a huge squealing pig, its blood spurting all over you. A man who could do that might be able to kill a girl, too.

FIFTEEN

BASURA

Dantan sat on their pleasant little balcony overlooking the lemon tree stuck in the hard baked ground. It was very early the next morning, before the heat would bear down uncomfortably. Judy was still sleeping. He would have very much liked a cup of strong steaming coffee but did not want to disturb her by having a waiter arrive at the room.

They would be departing soon. Judy and Miri had talked until they were hoarse, Judy had exhausted her shopping urges, at least for the moment, and Dantan himself felt he could do very little more to help determine Maria's killer, unless Jean-Jacques were to provide useful information from analyses he was doing in Paris.

The best thing about coming to Ibiza was that he and Judy had had a delicious "reunion," rediscovering why they had fallen in love with each other in the first place. The long afternoon *siestas* were made to order for love, and they got back in practice.

Whenever Judy was willing to leave for home, he was more than ready. He was not enamoured of the intense dry heat in San Marino, nor did not he believe he would uncover anything useful in the matter of the murder. True, he was awaiting results of forensic analyses of items he had sent to Jean-Jacques. But what difference could any of the results make if he had nothing else to grab onto?

One more time he would go over all that he had learned or suspected of the various possible suspects, in the hopes that his subconscious had been harder at work than had his conscious mind. Perhaps he would have a new insight.

As to the local men, Dantan ruled them out (apart from Tomas, who was still a suspect in his mind). He had not been able to unearth any motive. And there wasn't a breath of suspicion about any of them. A very far-fetched possibility was the coal-stoker at the *fonda*. He was the closest any of the local men had to opportunity, because he worked in the basement where Maria sometimes did laundry. He could have wheeled the body away in his barrow. But then there would surely have been traces of coal dust on the body, even if he had wrapped it first. No, Dantan did not suspect the coal-stoker.

Any of the local women? Rivalry among some of the maids? A strong woman could over-come the frail girl. But Dantan couldn't believe it. The local peasants were calm and resigned. It was not in their nature.

Ilse, the fonda owner, had a vile temper, and may have had experience with violence during the war. She might have become infuriated with Maria over something, and shook or strangled her, then transported her to Tomas' truck as "laundry" on one of the carts used by the *fonda*. But hadn't someone commented that Ilse wouldn't hurt an underpaid, overworked employee! It was said as a joke, but con-tained some truth. Ilse was a businesswoman first, before any headstrong tendencies she might have.

Among the expatriates Dantan ruled out all the British. None of them had had contact with the girl.

That left Max, Fred, Jorgen, Hugo, Claude, the latter three of whom had the most opportunity, as they lived at the *fonda*.

Max was brutal to his girlfriend. This was no secret. And Maria had cleaned house for Max from time to time. Furthermore, Dantan had been told that Maria had been present when Max threw Francine and her clothes out of his house into the yard. Could this have inflamed him sufficiently to actually kill the girl? Max kept saying he thought Tomas had actually done it. But there was no evidence to show that *Max* had done it.

Fred absolutely could not have done it. He was too much under the surveillance of his wife to have made the slightest move toward Maria, particularly since she was still an immature girl.

Jorgen had had ample opportunity while Maria did laundry near his basement studio. Jorgen was a powerfully built man and could have carried off anyone, not just a thin slip of a girl. He was known to have wrung the neck of more than one chicken when the cook at the *fonda* needed help. Jorgen could simply have carried her in a sack over his shoulder, the kind of sack he used for his gathering his rocks.

Claude? He was big enough and probably strong enough, but Dantan shrank from considering him at all. Because he was a compatriot? Or because he was too downright civilized?

Even Hugo, ungainly as he was, could have transported the body in the big basket on the back of his Vespa to dump it where it would cast suspicion on Tomas.

Hugo intrigued him. He had told a lie that in itself was inconsequential, but far from being an innocent misrecollection, might have had a hidden motivation. When Dantan had been making conversation with him and had tried indirectly to find out what the man had been doing the night that Maria was presumably killed, he said he had gone to the movies, like practically everybody else did on Sunday nights. Under prodding the movie that he had described was not the one that had been showing that night. He said the film he saw took place in a jungle, with swarms of marauding ants destroying a plantation.

When Dantan and Judy were having breakfast at their hotel with Miri that first day she gave them a run-down on possible forms of entertainment in San Marino. She had, of course, mentioned the Sunday night movies. It was one of the big events in town. And the movie she said had played the previous Sunday was "Knute Rockne, All-American." She didn't actually remember the title but had said enough for him to recognize it. He had seen it, with pleasure some time before, in Paris, with French subtitles.

Later Dantan had learned that the movie the Belge had described had actually played the week before.

But it could have been a slip of the memory.

Then again, it could still be Tomas Bonet who had murdered the girl.

Dantan had learned that Maria had confided to one of her friends that she was smitten with Catalina's brother. Could Maria have gone with him to his truck sometime that Sunday night, or had followed him in the morning, and something had triggered his intense anger, anger strong enough to wrench the living breath from the girl? Suppose she had informed him that she was pregnant? And he was the father. Or suppose that once she followed him, he pursued advances with her beyond what she would accept, and he became enraged that she had led him on.

He and Judy decided to have a light breakfast at the cafe instead of the usual sumptuous feast at their hotel. At Liberto's they encountered Claude, having coffee and buns with a slim very chic woman in a gray linen suit. She had a short coif and looked very French. She was. Claude introduced them. Her name was Denise. She was a friend of Claude's and had a travel agency in Paris.

"I lured Denise here to give the stamp of approval on San Marino as a location for a quality French restaurant!" Claude smiled.

"It sounded like a possibly intriguing place to send clients who want sun, beach, and drink, inexpensively."

"Well I was delighted when you decided to come down."

"I am intrigued to meet an Inspector of the *Police Judiciare*," Denise smiled. "How did you happen to choose to visit here, Inspector?"

Dantan was not about to admit that he had been requested to visit to see if he could help solve a local murder case, and that he had failed to do so.

"I have a friend who is an artist and came here to paint," Judy said brightly. "She wanted us to stay with her, but we decided to go to the Hotel Palma Linda, as Miri has no hot water. Her work is very good. I have some of it."

"How interesting," said Denise politely.

"She's done some beautiful scenes of San Marino," Judy went on.

"Really?"

Claude said, "Maybe you should take a look at them, Denise, you might find one you would like to hang in your office."

"A good idea." She turned to Judy. "Would you arrange a meeting for me with your friend to see her paintings?"

Judy bubbled at the request. She expected Miri and Seymour to come to Liberto's at around five. They could make the date then.

At five, Judy and Dantan came by taxi to Liberto's. Claude and Denise were already there. Miri and Seymour arrived soon after on foot. They were introduced to Denise.

Judy said, "Denise would like to see your paintings. I was telling her about the scenes you did of San Marino."

Denise smiled and nodded.

"Oh those," Miri said. "I'm working in a way now that I like better."

"But I liked those too," Judy said.

"You seem to like everything," Miri said contemptuously. "Jorgen said they looked like travel posters."

"Travel posters!" Denise exclaimed. "Perfect! Now I really want to see them."

"You do?"

"I'm a travel agent."

"But I've decided they're not that good."

"Maybe not as everlasting art," Denise smiled, "but maybe they would suit my travel office."

Judy whispered to Miri, "You might be more agreeable when someone might be interested in buying one of your paintings."

Throughout this discussion Seymour had been quietly smiling to himself. He seemed to enjoy Miri whatever she did or said.

"I propose," said Claude, "that we take a taxi to Miri's house, look at the paintings, then all go to Pedro's for an early dinner. Pedro's will accommodate us even before he opens for supper." The three women sat together on the ample back seat, Claude and Dantan on the jump-seats facing them, and Seymour sat in the front with the driver, who rattled on joyfully in Spanish whether anyone understood him or not. He had made more money in the week the Dantans were in San Marino than he had made all year.

Denise was effusive over the style of the Miri's house. She and Claude sat on one concrete bench by the fireplace, Dantan and Judy on the other opposite them. Seymour helped Miri move out each of the paintings, holding them up for display. She did not want to put them on her easel, on which was set a work in progress. An easel, she thought, would be pretentious for showing "travel posters".

"I like that," Denise said after each one. When she had seen the four paintings she asked Miri what she would charge.

Miri was silent for a moment. "I don't know. I haven't thought about selling them."

Judy said helpfully, "Fred, the one who dribbles like Jackson Pollack, asked a thousand dollars for one of his paintings."

"That's ridiculous," Miri scowled. "I told you that was way too much. You didn't agree to pay that, did you?"

"Alphie didn't like any of his paintings, so I'm not going to buy any regardless of the price."

"May I offer forty thousand French francs for one? And I would like to buy two."

That was about one hundred dollars each, Miri quickly calculated. "Okay." She smiled. "That will more than pay for a trip to Barcelona!"

"Splendid!" Everyone was pleased at the transaction, although Judy thought Miri had let them go for too little. But Miri was pleased at being offered anything at all for her work, and Seymour was ecstatic to hear that Miri would now go to Barcelona. He fully intended to pay both their expenses for the trip, but if having her own money to do so was what persuaded her, he wouldn't argue – for now.

Seymour would have to leave soon, too, and had promised Miri that if she would go with him to Barcelona, he would fly to Paris from there. They could go see the Gaudis she wanted to visit. Miri had not yet decided whether she would do this. As usual she was ambivalent when it came to Seymour.

It was a way of driving him crazy that he seemed to thrive on!

Denise selected the two paintings she wanted, and they were set aside for her against the wall. Then she impulsively stated that she would buy all four.

"No," Miri said. "That's too much. You would really get sick of them."

"Anyway," Judy said, "I want to buy one, too."

Denise demurred to the eccentric artist and her acquisitive friend. Claude said he would retrieve the ones Denise had chosen the next day.

Judy's faithful taxi driver was waiting at the road for them, and they piled in for the trip to the village.

First they stopped at Liberto's for more aperitifs, then eventually walked along the docks to Pedro's place. By then the sun had set and the sky was darkening.

That night the wharf was deserted. No fishermen were partying, no strollers ambled along the quay. And there were no other patrons in the restaurant. Even the bar frequented by fishermen, next to Pedro's place, was virtually deserted.

"It's creepy," Judy commented.

Claude, however, painted a verbal portrait of the place hung with colored party lights outside, music from a gramaphone – lilting French songs, of course – Jacqueline Francoise, Pierre Brasseur, Edith Piaf – Claude even sang snippets of their songs....

The meal was delicious and perhaps too satisfying. Before the cheese and fruit they all decided to take a stroll along the quay. It was now dark and still deserted, but the night was balmy, much of the heat of the day dissipated. As they walked they heard a rumbling behind them. It was a workman with a large cart with a foul-smelling load. The man, moving more rapidly than the group of friends, passed them, then stopped at a certain spot on the dock, where he summarily dumped the contents of his cart into the water, then rattled the empty cart back to the restaurant.

"*Basura*," said Claude. "Garbage."

"Ooh, that's disgusting," Judy said.

"Well they have to do something with it," Claude said. "And that's a deep spot, it will settle down.

A deep spot. A good place to dump a body, thought Dantan. Except that the night of the murder perhaps the culprit, intent on throwing the body into the water, came upon a raucous party going on at the fishermens wharf. Before being seen he could have turned around and dumped the body behind Tomas' truck, which would have hidden it from the fishermen's sight.

He told Claude, "I would like to question the 'garbage-man'". This was the only employee he had not questioned when he previously spoke with Pedro's staf.

Claude sought out Pedro and had a few words with him. The result was that Pedro brought the worker to their table to speak with Claude, but since the man spoke no Spanish, only Ibicencan, Pedro translated.

"Were you working the Sunday night the fishermen had a party at the wharf?"

"I'm always working."

"Did you dump garbage that night?"

"I dump it every night. Putrifies otherwise."

"Were there many people on the quays that night?"

"No one. Only the fat one with the motorscooter."

Miri gasped.

"Where did you see him?"

"As I was coming back from the pier, he was rumbling toward me a ways off, but before he got to the fishermen he turned around quickly and drove back from where he came."

"Did he stop anywhere?"

"I don't know. I wasnt paying much attention to him."

Dantan was stunned. He might have discovered the killer.

Dantan drew Seymour aside confide his new thought. Hugo could have had the girl's body in the basket on his scooter, and could have been intending to dump it in the water in the deep spot, but came upon the fishermen carousing and beat a fast retreat, seizing the opportunity of Tomas' truck to dump it out of sight before taking off.

Seymour agreed that it sounded plausible, but questioned whether the basket on the scooter was big enough to hold the girl's body.

"I'm going to take a close look at it as soon as I can," Dantan said, "but I believe so. She was such a little thing."

Claude suggested they all stop for a nightcap at Liberto's, which was full of other foreigners, the sounds of their merriment in direct proportion to the amount they had drunk already.

But the other two couples were ready to turn in and all said goodnight. The four climbed into Judy's taxi and rode together as far as the Dantans' hotel. Seymour insisted on keeping the taxi the rest of the way to Miri's house although she was upset at the cost.

Seymour pointed out to her that he could well afford it. Even though he was being discharged from the army at only a slight pay increase than that of the mere private he had started at, he had won a lot at poker and had saved a lot of his winnings.

After Dantan and Judy had climbed into bed and had had some pleasurable lovemaking, Dantan rose to sit contemplatively on their balcony. He had no proof that Hugo had committed the murder, but now he was morally certain that he had.

The garbage-man's "evidence" was too flimsy to be accepted by the law, particularly if the police were disinclined to suspect anyone other than Tomas. And there was no assurance that the witness would agree to repeat what he had seen to the police. He might be too intimidated.

So Dantan could do nothing.

SIXTEEN

REPORT FROM JEAN-JACQUES

Several days later, on Sunday morning, at the hotel, waiting around after breakfast, Dantan awaited the anticipated phone-call from Jean-Jacques.

"Anything doing at the P.J.?"

"Nothing. The *salauds* seem to have taken August off too! How are you enjoying yourself, *mon vieux*?"

Dantan gave a somewhat sardonic laugh, which his pal was free to interpret any way he liked.

Jean-Jacques proceeded to report the results from his forensic examinations. All the samples from the blankets at the fonda were virtually identical; same wool, washed in the same soap. One of the blanket samples – this Dantan determined from his chart was from the Belge's room – contained a thread which matched the sample from the black dress – the dead girl's. Threads from the various garments in the rooms revealed no useful information. The brown spot from the girl's dress proved to be a trace of chocolate.

"Thanks very much, *mon vieux*. We'll be returning to Paris very soon."

"Glad to hear it."

Although Dantan was now virtually certain that Hugo had murdered the girl, he knew that the report of Pedro's garbage-man, the only slightly suggestive evidence Jean-Jacques had analysed for him in Paris, was insufficient to interest the official Spanish investigators. Their only hope to get the local police interested was an explicit confession from the Belge. But why should he?

Maybe Nigel or one of the other foreigners who knew Hugo better might be able to think of a way to press the right button.

So while Judy was still sleeping – since it was Sunday and she could not go shopping, she would be staying in bed late – he put on his hiking boots, left his wife a note and walked off to the village.

Nigel was the only expatriate who had so far arrived at the cafe. He greeted Dantan heartily,

Dantan pulled up a chair beside him, signalled Liberto for a coffee, and proceeded to inform Nigel of what he had heard from Pedro's garbage-man.

"The first time I tried to ask questions at the establishments at the wharf nobody mentioned the garbage-man. I did get to talk with some of the fishermen who had been partying the night Maria died, but none of them recalled anything unusual. As for Pedro's staff, he had brought out his cook, his waiter, the scullery-maid, the coal-stoker.... Claude, who was doing the translating for me said that Pedro had assured him that they had covered everyone. But they hadn't, as it turns out. He had forgotten the one person who had seen anything that night."

"This garbage-man,' said Nigel. "He may be unwilling to relate what he saw to the police. A lowly Ibizan, can't even speak Spanish, won't want to get involved with the police. But what he told you sounds like it is Hugo."

That was Dantan's view too. "The analyses I received from Paris are not useful. Do any of your crowd know Hugo well enough – understand his psychology – to suggest how he might be persuaded to confess? But there's no reason he should. He's in the clear."

"He hasn't associated much with any of us. Not so much his choice as ours. Max can't stand him,

scornfully calls him the Belch, and the women shy
away from sitting near him. Except Harriet. Jorgen
might have some ideas, living in close proximity at
the *fonda*. Harriet might even have a thought or two,
she has taken pity on him and talks to him once in
awhile.

"Harriet is a thought. I'll speak with her later."

Others of the crowd had been drifting into
Liberto's. One of them was Jorgen. Nigel asked him
to come over to his place to talk. Jorgen agreed without asking for an explanation. Seymour arrived just
then. Miri had given him strict orders not to disturb
her that morning, she wanted to paint.

Nigel invited Seymour to join them. The four
men adjourned to Nigel's and Pamela's house. It
was small, a peasant's cottage in a field, furnished
with plain locally-made wood and rattan furniture.
Its main virtue was that it was close enough to the
village to be supplied with electricity, when the men
at the small plant chose not to play games with the
residents by turning the power off and on.

Pamela was up, floating about in a flowery
robe. She immediately announced that she would
be dressing and going out shortly, and would leave
them a pot of tea. "I'm going to call on Dorcas and
Hazel."

The men sat down around the square natu-
ral-wood dining-table that stood in the main room.

"Jorgen," Nigel said, "Dantan has probably discovered who the murder is. Hugo. But we don't have enough proof to go to the police."

"The Belge! How did you arrive at that conclusion?"

"A hypothesis, only," said Dantan, "not a certainty." He told Jorgen and Seymour what the garbage-man at Pedro's had related.

"And," Nigel said, "he would probably not repeat it to the police, just act as if he remembered nothing. But we've got to figure out something. Tomas may be living on borrowed time if the real killer is not revealed soon."

"Perhaps we could bribe Pedro's garbage-man to tell his story?" Jorgen suggested.

Nigel said, "Bribes from foreigners don't seem to work with these people. I know. I've tried in the past."

Jorgen asked Dantan, "You had collected evidence at the *fonda*, with the aid of the maid Consuelo. Catalina told me she had translated for you. What did you find?"

"It's true that analyses were done for me by a buddy in Paris of samples of matter taken from rooms at the *fonda* and from the dead girl's body and clothing. A snip from her dress matched a thread taken from a blanket in the Belgian's room. Not sufficient to be incriminating but could be indicative, was a small spot found on her dress of dried chocolate, a distant possibility that it was related to supplies of chocolate the Belgian kept in his room. Since the dead can't speak, and the perpetrator won't, we don't know if he offered her chocolate in his room. But he was known to offer the maids chocolate on other occasions.

"These items are not enough to take to the police. Nor would telling them what Pedro's worker reported, even if he were willing to repeat it. The worker hadn't noticed whether the 'fat man' stopped, say, near Tomas' truck, and dumped anything from the large basket on his Vespa. It is only a presumption on our part. It could be argued that it was a coincidence that Hugo was riding his Vespa on the quays that Sunday night. Without any body in his basket, without any nefarious purpose."

"What about the thread on his blanket which matched the girl's dress?" Nigel demanded.

"A thread or two could have been left just in the process of her cleaning his room."

"I say the Belge did it," Jorgen declared. "And we require him to confess. And write it down."

"I agree," Dantan said, "But why would he do that?"

Jorgen smiled broadly, and made a wringing

motion with his hands.

Seymour frowned. "Coercion would render any confession inadmissible."

"Coercion?" Jorgen echoed blankly. "No coercion. He will ardently desire to write his confession when I have persuaded him that it is best that he do so."

Nigel said, "We could promise him that we would not prevent him from leaving the island once he had handed over his confession. I don't care if he is arrested and punished or not, I only care that Tomas be definitively absolved."

Dantan said, "He won't be unless we get more evidence. Jorgen, hold off with any arm-twisting until I look into one more thing." Dantan had just had an idea. "Jorgen, that Sunday, when Maria was presumably murdered, you said that you had seen her around in the late afternoon scrubbing laundry?"

"Correct."

"What happened to the laundry? Did she hang it up outside afterwards?"

"That I can say she did not. The clotheslines are outside my windows. I would have observed her, or if not her, then the laundry hanging there later. Besides, the maids normally hang their laundry earlier in the day, when the sun would dry it. Not that there wasn't still sun in late afternoon, but I saw no clean laundry hanging."

"Did you then notice a basket of wet laundry when she was done?"

"I don't know when she finished. I didn't notice. But I would have noticed had there been a basket of laundry on the floor when I stopped working."

"So by the time you left your studio, Maria was no longer working there, and you saw no basket of laundry?"

"Correct."

"If she was doing personal laundry for one of the guests," suggested Nigel, "she may have taken the basket of wet clothes to the guest's room with the intention of collecting it in the morning to hang it up outside then."

"Why would she take it upstairs, wet?" Dantan asked.

Jorgen said, "Ilse sometimes becomes angry when she thinks the maids are using a lot of heated water for doing wash for guests, so the girls try to be discreet about it."

"But by the morning she was dead," Dantan said. So what happened to the wet clothes?" Nigel said.

That was exactly Dantan's point.

"Maybe Consuelo can help us find out," said Nigel.

Dantan was dubious. "Consuelo did a good job of collecting evidence, and intelligent as she seems to be, I don't think she is capable of questioning the other maids at the *fonda* to find out who might have done Maria's duties that morning two weeks ago or remember seeing something in one of the guest rooms then.."

"Catalina," Jorgen said. "Catalina knows everybody, speaks all the languages, is very bright."

"Good idea!" said Nigel. "I'll speak to her right away. At the *paseo.*"

"Do not trouble yourself," said Jorgen. "I will address the question with her myself. I am happy for a rationale to speak with her. I'll do so at the Bonets' store tomorrow morning."

"Suppose she learns nothing?" said Nigel impatiently. "Then what do we do?"

"What we would have done without further information," said Jorgen stubbornly. "Confront Hugo with what we have." He smiled. "And persuade him that it is in his best interests to provide a written confession."

Dantan was not going to debate this point until he saw what further information they could gather.

Pamela bustled in, noting that none of them had touched the tea. "You need a lady to pour for you?" she chided.

"You are an angel of mercy," Nigel smiled. "And how are the ladies you were visiting?"

"Hazel is quite atwitter that Miri is going to paint her portrait. It seems Miri did a lot of sketches on a recent visit."

"I hope Hazel won't be disappointed," Seymour chuckled. "Miri's so-called portraits of late have been unrecognizable as such."

"That would be a shame," said Pamela.

"But it might be better art," smiled Jorgen.

SEVENTEEN

LAUNDRY

Dantan puzzled over the laundry Maria had been doing the afternoon of the day she was murdered. If Jorgen's observations were accurate, then what had happened to the wet laundry? Jorgen had not seen her hanging it up in the yard, nobody had seen it at all. Ilse's maids did not do *fonda* laundry on Sundays, therefore it was likely that Maria had been doing the personal laundry of one of the guests. Had she delivered it wet to her customer, planning to hang it up the next morning? By which time, of course, she was dead. Or had she been startled by her attacker in the basement while she was doing the washing, and the attacker took the wet laundry away so as to remove a clue as to the time and location of the murder? If so, then what did he do with it afterwards?

Jorgen, obviously, had the greatest opportunity to attack Maria if the attack had occurred in the basement. But then why would he have mentioned her presence there at all, or the laundry, as it only underlined his opportunity, and raised the question of the laundry's subsequent disposal?

Dantan decided to try to find out which guests had their laundry done up the hill by the laundresses in their own establishment. By eliminating those people, he could arrive at a shorter list of *fonda* guests who might have been Maria's customers. He remembered that the day Seymour arrived and they were inspecting the *fonda,* they met the Belge on his way out with a big sack of laundry – or so he had said. Dantan haád put him down as a customer of the laundresses, and therefore not of Maria's. He would try to uncover the names of others.

He asked Miri to act as his interpreter. Together they climbed the hilly cobblestoned street laughing over the times in Paris when he was the English interpreter for the P.J. and she and Judy were both flirting madly with him.

The laundresses worked in a tiny immaculate storefront, the washing-room evident in the back through an open doorway. The counter and the floor of the tiny front room were piled high with folded white sheets awaiting their owners, basketsful of clothes and linens on almost every inch of the floor awaiting washing. A strong antiseptic smell permeated the place, no doubt emanating from the back where the tubs and wringers and irons were. A coal-stove was kept burning no matter how warm the day, as it was needed for boiling water and for heating the heavy cast-iron irons which had to be handled with cloths to protect the hand. As one iron was used and cooled too much to be useful, another was taken off the stove and the first one put back on it. If any of the girls could ever see and use an electric iron, Miri thought, they would think they had died and gone to heaven.

Dantan learned from one of the laundresses that a Frenchman, no doubt Claude, was a customer, bringing his personal laundry in weekly. They had no other regular customers from among the guests at the *fonda*, they thought the maids there did the laundry for many of the guests. The fat Belge from the *fonda* did come in infrequently. The last time, "sometime back," that he had come in he had brought in a basketful of laundry to be ironed. It was already clean – but soaking wet. She couldn't remember exactly when that had been.

This was sufficiently unique to persuade

Dantan that it was the Belgian's laundry Maria had been doing that Sunday. Suppose she had delivered it to him wet. He had tried to seduce her, perhaps trying to tempt her with chocolate, she had resisted and he had been clumsy or vicious, and caused her death. Later he carried the wet clothes to the laundresses up the hill.

Dantan told Nigel and Jorgen of his suspicions. Jorgen was more sure than ever that the Belgian had killed the girl. He promised the other two men that he would close the matter satisfactorily.

Jorgen cornered Hugo at next morning's breakfast at the *fonda*, followed him to his room, shoved him up against a wall with his large powerful hands threateningly around the Belge's fat throat, as he told him succinctly that it was known that he had killed the girl and that he would be turned over to the police with "their evidence" (he didn't say whose) after a thorough beating unless he penned a confession of how the killing had happened. This document would be held until he left San Marino in haste for Ibiza and the boat to Barcelona. Jorgen and his friends would let him go. After the Belge was safely away, on a plane to anywhere he chose on the Continent, away from Spain, they would then give the police the confession, so as to clear Tomas Bonet.

Jorgen was persuasive. The Belge was sweating, and quivering like a bowl of jelly. He scrawled and signed signed the confession, and handed it over to Jorgen, who waited there while the other man packed his bags. Jorgen escorted him to a taxi and got in with him, keeping a painful grip on the other's upper arm all the way to Ibiza city. He stayed very close to him until it was time to embark.

The two men walked side-by-side up the gangway, Jorgen always gripping the other's arm, then settled into deck-chairs side by side until the boat slowly moved out of its mooring and into the sea.

Jorgen was supposed to see him off the boat in Barcelona and onto a plane for Paris, staying closely with him at every moment. His captive, trembling violently, did not try to thwart or escape from Jorgen.

The next afternoon Nigel received a telegram from Jorgen: "He is gone."

When the usual crowd of expatriates, minus Jorgen and Hugo, was assembled at Liberto's cafe for the afternoon libations, Nigel imparted his news. The women, especially, were relieved that the murderer had been discovered, and dispensed with. But Max said gruffly, "He got off too easy."

Fred agreed.

Claude, while agreeing that Hugo had, while not exactly getting away with murder, got off too lightly, was relieved that there would be no scandal or much public talk, as it could have been bad for his business. He telegraphed Denise at her travel agency to inform her of the good news. She was somewhat relieved too, as she was coming down soon with another party of tourists, but she couldn't help but think that a little talk of murder would titillate the travellers and spice up their journey.

Harriet was the only one to feel at all sorry for Hugo: he could never return to Spain, and he would be haunted all his life by the memory of what he had done. So Harriet thought.

"I think once he's clear of us," said Max, "he'll go back to stuffing himself and he'll forget all about the whole thing."

"What do you think, Dantan?" asked Nigel. "Did we let him off too easy?"

"We did what we had to do, given the circumstances. And Jorgen," he added cryptically, "will do what he has to do."

Dantan and Judy left on the next boat for Palma, to fly to Paris from there. Seymour had to return to Paris before going with Miri to Barcelona, as his leave was up.

EPILOGUE

By the time Jorgen returned from Mallorca, Dantan and his wife had left for Paris. Jorgen gave Nigel a terse description of his journey with Hugo. Then the two of them went to the police with Hugo's confession, only letting them read it.

They had some difficulty persuading the police of the genuineness of the document, as it seemed unbelievable to them that someone would confess to murder unless he had been tortured. Jorgen and Nigel exaggerated their lack of fluency in Spanish to avoid getting into a detailed discussion.

After the local police had had time to confer with their superiors on the mainland, and get the original of the confession in their hands, they "lost interest" in Tomas Bonet. Coincidentally, this occurred simultaneously with sums changing hands among various strategic partipants.

It took Miri several weeks to make up her mind to actually go back to America. Her indecision arose every time she had another letter from Seymour, but she explained her delay by the fact that she had to pack her paintings, close her Spanish postal money account, and visit with each of the expatriates she had assiduously avoided during her stay.

Before departing from Spain, Miri shipped the paintings she had done on Ibiza to Judy in Paris, for safekeeping. Judy had excess space in her vast apartment and was glad to have them. She was already storing other paintings of Miri's, ones done in Paris. Once Miri had a third-class passage on a ship, and knew from which port it would be sailing, Judy would pack and ship them to her there.

Seymour had already flown back to the States, transportation provided by the U.S. Army. He was looking for a low-rent cold water flat on Manhattan's Lower East Side for her. He had already found a studio apartment on the Upper West Side for himself, and had gotten an apprentice job in a law office.

About two months after she had settled back in New York City, and was enthusiastically painting at the Art Students League and just as enthusiastically rollicking between the sheets with Seymour on weekends, Miri received a letter from Mavis in San Marino. Miri's stay there seemed far away by then.

"Dear Miri --

"I hope this letter finds you well and happy, and enjoying whatever you're doing.

"Some news of San Marino I thought you might want to hear. A body has been fished out of the Mediterranean Sea near the port of Palma de Mallorca which the authorities think may be our own Belge! Here's the quote now from the newspaper: 'A male body has been retrieved from the sea near the port of Palma de Mallorca which has been tentatively identified as Hugo Klaus, 29, a Belgian national who had been residing on Ibiza, in San Marino. This gentleman booked passage from Ibiza to Palma on August 26. Coroner reports that estimated height and weight of corpse approximate what is known of Hugo Klaus.'

'Justice est faite!

"Catalina Bonet and Jorgen have gotten engaged! and have gone to Stockholm on a freighter carrying Valencia oranges, to get married. They kept their secret until the last moment. Jorgen paid for their passage with a piece of sculpture for the head of the shipping line who had heard about him from one of the dentists who were supporting Jorgen here in exchange for pieces of sculpture. Catalina was

very sly. None of us had an inkling until just before
they left for Sweden. Tomas is going to fly up to
Stockholm for the wedding, but the parents are not
going. Probably because of the expense. Harriet
thinks maybe because they are unhappy that not
only is Catalina is marrying a foreigner but will live
far away in another country. I think Tomas would
like to do the same!

"On a sad note, we have had another funeral
for a young girl. That makes two this year. This one
is the daughter of Teresa, one of the peasants who I
believe worked for you. Very sad. Vicente said the
girl had been languishing for years, with an unknown
illness.

"As for me, Vicente and I are still together
and I suppose always will be as long as I stay on
Ibiza. He couldn't be transplanted anywhere else.

"I have broken ground for my new house,
but still have misgivings about building here. I'm so
worried that the place will change. If it doesn't work
out I'll sell and go elsewhere. I do want to stay,
though, because of Vicente. He couldn't survive
anywhere else.

"There are a lot of foreign buyers around
looking for little houses, more than ever. Your house
is very much in demand, but the drunken agent has
boarded it up and refuses to show it. He thinks you

were the only foreigner he ever met who was worthy of living there! We sit around over drinks sometimes trying to figure out why. We did finally find
out that the owner is an old man now who lives in
Barcelona with the daughter who disgraced him in
that house years ago (probably by doing once what
we do here all the time). The place is anathema to
its owner, but that doesn't prevent the agent from
treating it like some sort of shrine. That was why he
kept it closed up.

"Nigel is still hankering for that house, but is
worried too about the signs of boom. There are
many:

"1. Claude has purchased Pedro's restaurant
and has alreeady started refurbishing it. Pedro stays
on as one of the cooks and has a small piece of the
ownership, no doubt to ensure his staying on. Claude
himself plans to cook the French items that will be
offered.

"2. Denise has brought several large tour
groups to San Marino, and she has them staying at
the *Fonda Bahia.* Ilse has managed so far to suppress
any visible signs of hatred for the French, as they
are spending generously at her place. The French
tourists are also big customers for the nuns' embroidered christening gowns. Francine, with her shy and
gentle manner, has helped Denise out by taking

small bands of her female tourists to see the nuns. Denise has been trying to persuade Francine to come back to Paris with her to work in her travel agency, and it looks like it might happen, which would be the best thing Francine could do, leave Max for good.

"3. Even the nuns are going commercial! They are sewing exquisite baby clothes on spec!

"4. Max has bought the house he was renting and is excavating for a swimming-pool.

"5. There is still talk at Hotel Palma Linda of building a pool. And the bay is so crystalline!

"Harriet is still here but is talking about going to the Far East. She had a letter from the young couple who had trekked off to the gurus, and got all fired up about Buddha.

"Fred sold a huge painting to a female German tourist, a gorgeous Valkyrie with thick blonde hair in coils, and he is now cock-of-the-walk. The rumor is that he slept with her in the course of the negotiations over the painting. Cindy is ambivalent over the sale. She has less control over Fred since this success, but she likes the money.

"Do write, and best regards, Mavis."

Miri wrote to Judy about the news of the discovery of Hugo's body in the sea.

Judy replied promptly. She had news of her

own: "I'm expecting! Alphie is delirious.

"As for the Belch, Alphie had always suspected that Jorgen wouldn't let him escape retribu-
tion merely by signing a confession and then disappearing.

"Alphie sends his best to you and Seymour,
and hopes you will make it back to Paris sometime.
Naturally we would expect the two of you to stay
with us. But I'll probably see you in New York first.
I have no intention of having my baby in a French
hospital, where the nuns will let you die if it's a
choice between you and the child. So I'm going to
have the baby in Long Island Jewish Hospital. My
mother is so relieved at that. I hope I'll be able to
pry the baby loose from her when it's time to return
to Paris!

"Please stay in touch. -- Love, Judy"

* * *